PETE B

SEX

and the

DEATH

of

CHIVALRY

@iamselfpub
www.iamselfpublishing.com

WHAT HAPPENED LAST NIGHT?

When I awoke, I had a massive pounding in my head.

The flat was littered with broken glass and pictures were scattered across the laminate. The new pair of heels I'd bought for her lay on the floor next to me, along with the photo. Our photo.

One of the heels was straight through my eye, tearing the picture. We'd taken it beside the river the first night we met. I had always loved how amazing her feet looked in those, with her toes painted and beautifully manicured. However, lying there, with one of them maiming my half of the photo they somehow didn't seem quite as elegant as they once did.

The sunlight shot through the window and beamed across the broken glass like a stone skimming the water of a lake. It almost blinded me… as if my head wasn't throbbing quite enough already.

Being so hungover still, it was impossible to picture what the hell had happened the night before; all I could think about was just how much my head hurt and… who the fuck was going to clean the flat!?

As I stumbled around, anxiously trying to find my phone, I casually overlooked the mess that lay before me. I proceeded to exercise a hangover cure, whilst swigging from a half-empty bottle of Jack.

I am Harrison and this is my life; surrounded by half-empty bottles, broken glass and a hangover from hell. You may say it's screwed up, but hey, it works. I'm just trying to keep it together, whilst everything else seems hell-bent on falling apart.

Knowing Lilly the way that I did, I thought it would be best to leave her to simmer for a while. If she was that angry, it normally lasted the duration of the day.

Once I had figured out where my phone was amongst the rubble, I noticed there was a text from Joe. He wanted to meet for breakfast. Why not? The mess isn't going anywhere; the flat will still be an Absolute state when I get back, right?

Joe was an old friend from university and I'd not seen him in a while. I always enjoyed hanging with him; you would never know how the night would unfold, really. There was always the potential for something interesting – or disastrous – to happen. Either way, it was never going to be boring, that's for sure.

As I was leaving the flat, I thought I had stumbled across some sort of contemporary art gallery for a moment. Besides all the broken glass and photos strewn across the floor, it looked as though someone had done a number on the wall too, Picasso style. There was a very artistic, yet angry, inscription that read 'ASSHOLE' in bright red lipstick across the whole width of the wall by the door to the flat.

The town was bustling, as it always was on a Saturday. As you got closer to the river, the rich aroma of street food vendors filled the air, from Thai to a real classic, a real favourite of mine: the bacon-cheeseburger.

Still, it was not really my first choice for a hangover cure.

A Bloody Mary and a coffee would slowly bring me back to life, working as a chaser for my JD aperitif.

We met up in our favourite spot, the Benedict, along the south bank. The place was always busy, maybe because it was designed like an American diner; it had long booths, and a menu to die for: pancakes and bacon and eggs benedict – as the name would suggest.

"Good to see you, Joe. How are you, man?"

"I'm great, Harrison. What's going on?"

I could see the glazed yet nonchalant (somehow flickering with nervousness) look in Joe's eye. I had a feeling something was up. Having known Joe for a long time, I knew that he had huge heart, but also that he was slightly lacking in confidence. He always had to work that little bit harder to get what he wanted, but he would never succumb to giving up.

"You don't look too hot yourself, though…" Joe mused.

"Ha ha, you're not wrong, Joey boy. I had a bit of a heavy night with a few of the boys from work yesterday, but I'm just about holding on, for now."

Damn, do I really look that bad? I feel ok. Maybe I'm still drunk and I just can't tell?

We grabbed ourselves a table by the window, so we could sit and watch the world go by.

The hostess glided her way over to us, I thought of ordering for Joe too, but decided against it; I don't need to be getting anyone else's back up today. I let him have his say, and we sat and relaxed for a while before deciding how to tackle the day while putting the world to rights.

I prayed the caffeine injection would help bring me back to life.

"She's a sight for sore eyes, isn't she, Joe?"

"You say that as if you're back on the market again!?"

He replied, with a childish, cheeky tone, "No, not at all, Joe. It's just her long jet-black hair, the way she carries herself, looking so confident and proud. Reminds me of someone I know."

"Sure, Harrison I'm with you."

There really was something about that girl too, the way she walked and how she looked so perfect… and with minimal effort too.

"It's funny you should say that, though. We did have a bit of a row last night, Joe, from what I can vaguely recall. The flat looks like a scene from a war film right now. Nothing a good interior decorator couldn't fix, though, or maybe I'll attack it with the Henry later this afternoon."

"Nice," Joe replied. "Controversial as ever then."

It really was pretty horrific too. I'd seen tidier student houses than the post-apocalyptic mess that I'd woken up to this morning.

"Yeah, you could say that, Joe," I said. "So, what's new with you anyway? I've not seen you in a few days. Is everything ok with you and your lady? Aren't you supposed to be moving in a few weeks?"

"Yeah, Harrison, that's right. Only a couple of weeks now."

Now, that was great news!

As our eyes peered around the restaurant, watching all the people enjoying themselves and talking about the previous night, it seemed I wasn't the only one nursing a hangover. There were a few fragile-looking folk nursing themselves back to life that Sunday a.m.

Damn, I love this city. That's one of the many things we have always enjoyed about hanging out in the morning after a night on the town – always having a story to tell.

"Well, she doesn't seem to be entirely convinced that I'm 100% committed, which is odd, considering it was my idea to move in," Joe said as he let out a sigh. "Not to mention the fact that, even after two years, I'm still as in love with her as I was on the day we first met. She knows that I'm 100% on board with the idea, and after looking at six different places, we finally found one that is truly beautiful. It overlooks the water, has a nice little balcony too, and it's not far from the flat that she shares with her uni friend at the moment. You would think that would make for a nice and painless transition at the very least, commute-wise."

"The place sounds ideal, Joe." I said, hoping that Joe would make the right decision with their future in mind. "Have you signed any contracts yet? I'm guessing you must be about to if you only have a few weeks left, right?" I'll be honest, there aren't many that would sacrifice the shitty commute just to appease their woman.

"Well, yeah, that's the kicker, really," he replied. "We're literally on the cusp of signing and now it seems as if she's getting cold feet."

"You really need to be sure too. It really is hard work, and one hell of an adjustment."

The hostess returned with our drinks.

Ah sweet caffeine – quite possibly my favourite narcotic. Second only to alcohol.

"It's difficult, Joe. Trust me. I've been where you are." And I really had too. "I know how daunting it can be moving in with your partner. It's a huge step to take together, and for some couples, it really is the thing that makes or breaks them. You just need to wait until she's in a nice approachable mood. Preferably one where you won't need your helmet for fear of flying shrapnel."

If Lisa is already nervous, Joe's probably better off giving her some time to think about it on her own, rather than setting fire to the whole plan altogether.

"So how was last night anyway, Harrison?" Joe asked, changing the subject. "Where did you and the boys end up?"

"Ah, you know, nowhere particularly special," I replied. "Just the Final Final, in the city. The crazy thing about last night was that I wasn't even that keen on going out. Somehow, I managed to roll in at 3am, though! Still, it was a brilliant night – totally worth it. I'm pretty sure that the guys had a great time too. Jay threw up on the bar too! Mike wasn't too impressed, and I'm sure my laughing as he mopped it up didn't help the situation too much. He threw me out around two. It's a shame you weren't there too – really, you would have laughed your ass off."

"Ah Harrison, man, it sounds bloody hilarious. I bet Jay's suffering a little this morning."

"Yeah, I can imagine he would be," I said. "I've not heard from him yet. He's probably collapsed in a pile of drunken mess on the sofa. I might check in with him later, see if he's still alive, you know? It reminds me of our days at Cambridge – late nights and not knowing whose bed we would end up in!"

"Ahh, Cambridge… those were some great times, Harrison. Don't know how we managed to ever get anything done, considering our love for alcohol far out-weighed our desire to bury our heads in the books."

"You make a good point, Joe – still we made it, eventually."

"So, what's up with you and Lilly? You said you had some sort of row last night?"

"I'm not too sure really. I'm still trying to mentally piece it all together myself, you know? I'm guessing she was very pissed with me, as she did one hell of a number on the flat."

"Oh really?"

"Yeah, Joe. I woke up to one hell of a mess this morning (from the sofa I may add). Broken glass, pictures scattered around. You could say 'the writing's on the wall.'"

"Sounds a little too profound for a Saturday a.m. for my liking, Harrison."

"Literally. She actually scrawled 'ASSHOLE' in lipstick by the door to the flat."

"Shit, Harrison, you might have hit some sort of nerve there, I think. *Sofa* too, you said?"

"Yeah, Joe. Never a good sign, but not uncommon. It wouldn't be the first time I've slept on the sofa; we've been together a while now, so it happens from time to time, you know? The rest of it, though, was a bit disturbing; she must really be at boiling point."

As crap as it was not lying next to hurricane Lilly, the sofa was actually pretty comfy, albeit I froze my ass off on the leather.

"If you could have seen the flat," I continued. "It was quite a harrowing thing to wake up to. Almost like a murder scene, but instead of someone's blood, there was red wine all over the laminate floor."

"Well, I can't say that sounds good. I bet you must be anxious to get home then?"

"Can't say that I am, really, but someone's gotta clean the flat, right?" It would be good to get back, close the books on this and figure out a way to fix whatever has broken after last night, other than our photographs, and a few glasses.

The hostess returned with the food. "Here you go, fellas. Is there anything else I can get for you?"

"No thanks," I replied. "I think we're all set."

Joe nodded. "Well, I really hope you get the chance to fix things with Lilly, Harrison. You two are normally great when you're together."

"Thanks Joe, I hope so too."

He was right too. When we weren't tearing each other's eyes out, we were – for the most part – inseparable.

"I reckon I have a few hours before Lilly comes home," I said. "What do you say to a few drinks after we've finished here? Hair of the dog, so to speak. Might pick me up, and bring me back to life, slightly."

"Sure thing, Harrison. That sounds cool. Lisa isn't back from work for a few hours, so I'm at a loose end myself right now. Where were you thinking? The Loch?"

"Joe, you read my mind! I was thinking the same thing – my favourite place to recover with a few quiet ones after a nice heavy night."

"Awesome. Sounds like a plan, bud!"

"You think Lisa will come around, Joe?"

"I think so. It's just around the corner from the one she shares right now, so it's handy for her. I actually preferred the last place we looked at right before this one. It adds about fifteen minutes on to my commute, but I know that it makes her life easier…"

"That's very sweet, Joe," I said. "Sounds pretty gallant of you too – a dying breed, you might say. I don't remember the last time either Lilly or I felt that connected. Things haven't been too great lately, probably something to do with last night's events, if I had to guess."

Joe waved to the hostess and gestured for the bill. "I got this, Harrison. You can get the next one."

"Thanks. You know I got you covered."

The Loch was only a short walk from the Benedict, which was nice as the weather looked as if it might turn quite soon. The last bloody thing I needed was for the damn sky to open up and piss all over me. After my morning, that would just add insult to injury. At least Joe's here, we can get drunk and soaked together.

We arrived at the Loch, the stale smell of last night's alcohol and food still stained the floor and the smell was pouring out into the street. *Mmm, take it all in, Joe. What a beautiful place.*

We smiled at each other as we walked in. You can't beat a good little dive bar. The place had everything – high bar stools, a jukebox, a popcorn machine, and old photos all around the room from all the famous people that had visited the place over the years.

From starving artists to musicians, the place was always packed full of creativity. You could feel it as soon as you walked in the room...

The place had real character.

It truly was a great place; it had sticky floors, a vast selection of drinks, and food from English classics like pie and chips to BBQ chicken wings and fries.

As we made our way to the bar, amongst all the smells and memorabilia on the walls, there was something shiny that caught my eye. *It was Amy.*

Now I used to know Amy from a long time ago, from back when we were kids. We had always hung out after school and did everything together, from playing in the park to going away with each other's families for weekend breaks. She looked even more beautiful than I could ever remember, the last time I had laid eyes on her was just before I left for university.

Amy ran around the bar and jumped up straight into my arms, giving me a huge hug as she wrapped her legs around me. Her hair smelt incredible, like fresh cinnamon. She had the most beautiful green eyes too; they really brightened up the place, and me. I could quite easily lose a day in them.

She was wearing a tight black top with an electric guitar made of sequins. Her red leather trousers and cute little pair of black ankle boots complemented the look, and her dark brown hair fell perfectly just before the small of her back. That was one of the best things about Amy; she always managed to look incredible, so seductive and all, without spending all day in front of the mirror.

"Hey hot stuff, how the hell are you doing? Harrison, you look like shit!"

Just as polite as I remembered her.

"Thanks Amy," I laughed, whilst gently massaging my temple in a poor attempt to sooth my hangover.

Amy and I caught up briefly whilst she laughed at my misfortune of having to sleep on the sofa. Something in her eyes told me she was pretty keen to catch up.

"So, what have you two boys been up to, anyway? I've not seen you in what feels like a lifetime!"

What have I been up to? Trying to get a grip on the whole adult thing, one day at a time.

"I know, Amy," I replied. "It must be about four years, I guess." I sighed at that. "Nothing too exciting, just working really, and living with a girlfriend who I'm certain would love nothing more than to erase me like a bad carpet stain. Pretty peachy other than that, though. How about yourself, Amy?"

"Same here, Harrison; all work and no play makes Amy very sad. Aside from the boyfriend, though, it's just me and my cat, Lex, right now."

"I think it's probably best, Amy, sometimes, to save yourself for the convent. Or at the very least, become a lesbian. I hear that girls are a lot easier to be with than men."

"Oh, Harrison, you aren't all bad, you just fuck up. It's not your fault – our brains are just more evolved."

Painful as it was to admit, even to myself, I think she was right. Maybe someone should do a study on men's brains, and maybe they could determine how and why we systematically sabotage ourselves. That's a question for another time, though, I guess.

"Thanks Amy," I said. "I feel so educated right now."

I let out a sigh, in a poor attempt to try and hide the fact that I was kind of on-board with her idea.

"You're welcome, ass face. What can a girl say? The path to enlightenment is long. Tequila, boys?"

"Yeah, maybe just leave us the bottle."

"Well," Amy smiled, "this could get interesting."

"Ha, I don't think we're far off. Are we, Joe?"

"Yeah Harrison, I can't say that I disagree right now, but it's probably not the best of ideas. Or is it?"

We both elected not to go for the tequila, just yet, and decided on a beer.

"This is on me, guys. You both look as though you could use a friend right now."

"Thanks Amy. That's sweet of you, I owe you one."

We made our way to our favourite corner booth, by the window.

"You're on, loser!" Amy yelled back.

I'd really enjoy that too. Amy was always such a great listener and was always there for me when I needed to have a good bitch, but more importantly than that, she could give me some female perspective. She always understood me too, like nobody else could. Probably why I always gravitated towards her whenever she was around.

I always enjoyed the corner booth. Perfect for people-watching too. The calm before the storm, if you like.

"Ah, man, I really love this place, Joe," I said. "A beautiful little hideaway from the main part of the city. Busy, but not chaotic, you know?"

"Yeah man, it's a really cool joint too. I love all the guitars and photos on the walls. It kinda makes you think what this place would have been like in the 60s."

"I reckon it would have been bloody amazing, Joe! If I've learned anything from my vinyl collection, and television, it is that it was packed full of drugs, promiscuous sex, and incendiary guitar riffs."

"Surviving Cambridge was tough enough," Joe laughed. "I'm not sure we could have beaten the 60s though."

We both nodded and laughed. "I don't disagree," I replied. "I gotta say, though, Joe, it does sound as though you've stuck your neck out a little for Lisa. You could have been selfish and said 'fuck it' and stayed where you were. Yes, it will cost her a little more in rent, but you will both be there together, and that's all that counts, man."

"Thanks Harrison, I hope you're right too," Joe said. "So what's up with you and Amy then? She seemed to have a look in her eye as if she would have eaten you alive over there."

"Ha ha, did she?" I replied. "I didn't really notice, to be honest. I was too pre-occupied with not trying to throw up, and I was sort of zoned out for a moment. Quite surprised I didn't drop her, actually, although she's nice and light. Well, I mean you know we have a little bit of history, I guess, from before I went to university, although things never really took off, if I'm honest. Not for lack of trying, though, but people drift apart and change, and move on, you know?"

"Yeah, I'm with you, Harrison, but at least you have Lilly."

Oh yes, her. I can only imagine what lies in wait for me when I get back to the flat later this afternoon.

"You must be looking forward to heading back then."

Thinking about it, she had always been pretty down to earth. I sometimes ask myself how I managed to get myself into a different kind of situation each week.

"It won't be my favourite way to spend my Sunday afternoon, that's for sure, Joe," I replied. "We shall see, though. I suppose there can only really be a few possible scenarios; either there's a few suitcases loaded and ready to go by the door, she's sitting there in silence waiting for me to get back and launch a full-scale assault on my eardrums, or she's out getting smashed with her girlfriends."

I paused to think for a moment

"I just hope she can let herself calm down just enough to try and talk to me. Annoying as she can be sometimes, I'm not sure what I would do without her."

"Well, you could start by telling her that, Harrison. I mean, if she isn't throwing kitchen utensils at you, that is. I can lend you my crash helmet, just in case there's still some fallout in the atmosphere?"

"Joe, you've known me for way too long my friend."

God, I sound so dry, and deflated. Even I can hear it.

"Yeah, you're probably right, Harrison – longer than I'd care to remember!"

I gestured towards my empty glass, hinting at Joe to grab another one. Luckily, he got the hint and made his way over to Amy.

The bar was getting pretty busy now. I really had to applaud the daytime drinkers – if they're anything like us two they'll probably be out for the duration.

While I sat there waiting for Joe to get back from the bar, I felt someone grab my arm and I heard a familiar voice scream at me as my heart began to race.

"WHAT THE FUCK DID YOU SAY TO MY SISTER, HARRISON!?"

HELLO DRAMA, MY OLD FRIEND

IT WAS CRAIG, LILLY'S BROTHER.

Now Craig was, literally, the epitome of a big dumb animal. He had no job, no ambition, and looked like he spent the time most of us would be sleeping, in the gym.

Overly pompous, he loved talking about himself, but there wasn't a lot other than tumbleweed inside his cranium really.

"Well Craig, that's between Lilly and I, now isn't it?"

I could almost see where she gets it from now.

Best not to throw more petrol on the fire and verbalise that one, I reckon.

Not when he was already at tipping point. All I wanted to do was nurse my hangover and have a few more quiet beers with Joe.

"Not when it concerns me it doesn't, Harrison!"

He quickly raised his arms and went to lunge at my throat. I managed to just dodge him, whilst trying to get behind him so I could have the upper hand, and put him in a chokehold, so he wasn't able to do any serious damage.

While this was all unfolding, Joe and Amy came running over to try and break us up before things really turned bad. Now, I didn't particularly like violence, but I always like to have the last word if I can, especially with someone like Craig. There was no way I was about to get my ass handed to me in my favourite watering hole.

"Oi, calm the fuck down NOW!" Amy yelled at the both of us.

Amy had come running out from behind the bar with a 12-inch blade and edged it closer to Craig's throat. His enthusiasm seemed to deplete pretty rapidly at that point.

"FINE, I'll leave, but you haven't heard the last of this, Harrison. Not yet."

Craig had made sure he gave me a shove as he made his way out of the bar, nearly knocking over the other hostess. As he walked, he ignored everything around him, other than what was going on in his own tiny mind.

"He seemed nice, Harrison. Friend of yours?" Amy shook her head in disgust.

"Yeah, Amy, we're best buds, we are. That was Craig, Lilly's brother."

I see word travels fast. I wonder what else he may have caught wind of.

"So are you boys getting another beer? Or are you going to upset some more of my customers?"

"I'd love one please, Amy. Thanks for a minute ago too; my rock chick in shining armour – that was sweet of you."

I don't know how I felt about that really, being saved by Amy. Kind of indifferent, really, or just embarrassed. Either way, we managed to survive unscathed.

Amy let out a smile and winked at me. Cheeky. "You're welcome, dumb ass."

Amy poured two of the same.

I took a nice long sip of my beer and took a moment to collect myself.

"Just your average Saturday morning, eh Joe?"

Just as I had suspected, always some kind of action going on, Saturday, or whatever.

"Of course, Harrison, I wouldn't have it any other way really. Maybe a little less drama though? Although it does tend to follow you as of late, right?"

"Doesn't it just? I'm sorry you were caught up in that too, Joe. I know you have your own stuff to deal with and I don't want you being dragged down in my crap."

I really didn't want that for him either. I don't want any conflict with one of the few real friends I have left. Joe has his own stuff going on, and it's not right to expect too much of him.

"Don't worry about it, Harrison, sometimes these things can't be helped, I guess. That was nice bumping into Craig too, wasn't it? He seemed like a stand-up guy."

"I can't for the life of me think what might have upset him though," I replied. "I'm pretty certain that, if I drink a coffee or two and maybe sober up, just a teeny bit, I might be able to solve said mystery, young Joseph."

"I hope that you do," he said. "It doesn't seem as though it's been the best of hangover days for you today."

"No, it hasn't really, and I can safely say that I've certainly had some better in my time. So, how are you feeling about the whole Lisa thing, Joe? Are you gonna be ok when you see her?"

"Yeah, man. I mean, I think so. I'm sure we can manage to sort this out and come to some amicable resolution with minimal conflict, y'know?"

"You'll be fine, Joe. All you have to do is just listen to her." *I say, as if I've mastered her mind like some female mind Jedi.*

"I know that I've already said this to you before," I continued, "but let me reiterate (just because I know that you absolutely *love* the sound of my voice so much). Lisa knows that you're a fucking amazing guy with a hugely complicated job, and a very successful career, and you're one of the most grounded people I have ever met. Ever. You're not too ugly either. However, aside from saying all of this, which in your heart you should know, and without falling victim to your own vanity, we're forgetting one very crucial little plot point here: Lisa *already* knows this, all of it, so try not to worry about it, Joe. Everything will be fine, man."

Joe smiled and nodded in agreement.

All of this, of course, is true. Joe is a great guy, and one of the top architects in the city, working for one of the best firms in the city, Stribling and Jones. I, however, am working at the city university teaching aerospace engineering to a few lucky, but very clever, students. I really mean that too; to get on to my course you had to score 85% or higher on your entry exams. Not to sound too vain or narcissistic, but the test is incredibly hard. I only got 98% myself, so it's not for the faint of heart.

"Hey Harrison, what do you think Lilly is up to right now?"

"Who knows, Joey boy? I should probably head back soonish, though, I think. 'Fix bayonets', so to speak."

"Let's hope it isn't as bad as last night, Harrison."

Fuck, I really hope that things don't go down the way they did last night. I don't know how much more I can take sleeping on that damn sofa.

"Thanks Joe," I said. "Well, it's gotta happen at some point, I guess. I'll keep you posted though, bud. I had better check the heater in my car is working too. I could be sleeping in that shit-piece later tonight."

"Ha, well, let's hope not buddy – the sofa is a much safer bet."

"Dick! You're right though, at least that way I'm indoors, right Joe?"

"True indeed, and nobody will try to kid-nap you."

"Doubtful, Joe, you've met me, right?" I replied. "They'd probably give me back after about an hour, and most likely *pay me* the ransom."

"Yeah, that sounds about right actually, Harrison."

The bar seemed pretty desolate after our little rendezvous with Lilly's brother, Craig, earlier that afternoon. All the Saturday drinkers must have been feeling the pinch. Either that or perhaps they were heading home to some disgruntled partner too? Possible, I guess.

Amy, of course, was still working her shift. The sassiest and most elegant barmaid a boy like me had ever known.

Joe headed back to the bar to grab us another refill.

I probably shouldn't drink too much today, but something tells me that the night isn't going to get any better than this afternoon, so why not sink a few while catching up with my old buddy from uni?

"Do you ever think about what may have happened if you and Amy had got together, Harrison?"

"Sometimes Joe, yeah."

"Don't get me wrong though," Joe added. "Amy is fucking incredible, but she is only a mirage really. She's part of your past, and that's important, but you can't let it rule your present. What happened before may help to make you a better person, or worse. But you can't let it take hold of you. Now, that isn't to say something might happen in the future; somewhere along the line, but right now, you have to move forward and try not to look back. If you two do manage to find your way back to each other then you may find just what you've been searching for all along."

"Well Joe, who knew you could be so profound and talk so much sense with less than ten pints?" I rolled my eyes, suggesting that he really underestimated himself. "In all seriousness, though, I really appreciate you being there for me, man."

"Don't be stupid, Harrison. I will always be there for you. It's important to have a good ear sometimes, man. I know that you're stubborn as hell, but it's *ok to ask for help* sometimes, man."

"Thanks Joe, that means a lot."

We decided that was enough beer for today, and parted ways.

Just as we were saying our goodbyes to Amy, it began to pour down with rain.

Beautiful. What a perfect insult to add to my already incredibly salty day. Normally, I wouldn't mind the rain, but this time something bothered me. Whenever it rained on the weekend, Lilly and I would always cuddle up together on the sofa and just watch it for hours. She always loved the way the windows misted up, and the way the air smelt afterwards, like everything was all cleansed away, starting afresh again.

It was greyer than normal out and still hammering it down. I'd already been drinking, albeit without her, and she was already mighty pissed off with me. The cuddling would not be on the agenda, either on the sofa or anywhere else for that matter.

Man, this weather is not letting up at all.

I really hope the fucking bus turns up soon, I'm freezing my ass off here.

Although, I'm pretty sure Lilly would love that image: me freezing my ass off, with no jacket, and getting soaked.

Finally, my bus arrives.

Full of people too, brilliant. Looks like I'll be standing for the duration.

WHY SO TENSE, LISA?

So many unanswered questions

Slightly hypothermic, I arrived back at the apartment building. The lift was out too.

I'm only on the sixth floor not the twelfth so that's manageable, barely.

"Hey Lisa, so glad you're home!"

"Don't 'hey Lisa' me! Where the fuck have you been, Joe?"

Maybe I should have stayed in the pub with Harrison after all. Things were certainly more tranquil there. And they had beer.

"What do you mean, *where have I been*? You've been at work, haven't you?"

"Well, the flat is an absolute state!"

"Yes, yes it is, Lisa, and what's your point exactly? This is my flat, not yours."

"That's not the point, Joe."

Tell me, Lisa, what is the point according to your gospel?

Damn, if this is what she's going to be like when we move in, things could get interesting. I say interesting, what I really mean is, turn into a nightmare.

"Harrison and I had a pretty good afternoon, for the most part. I was actually out with him for breakfast, if you're really that interested, Lisa."

"The point is, Joe, that you're not on your own anymore. You can't afford to be lazy."

"First of all, Lisa, I'm perfectly aware that I'm no longer on my own. I am acutely aware of the fact that the two of us are one package and I wouldn't have it any other way."

"You went to the pub too?"

"Yeah, hun. Harrison had a pretty rough night and needed an ear, you know?"

"Not good. Bit of a blackout session, was it? That doesn't sound like the Harrison we know!"

"I know, right?" I replied. "As cool as Harrison is, though, it's you I want to be with. I love you more than him."

"Glad to hear it, Joe," she said. "And remember that nobody does that thing you like in bed the way I do!"

"I should certainly hope not, I'd be very worried. Not least for the sake of Lilly!"

Mmm, Lisa really did have many talents too, inside and out of the bedroom.

"So why are you home from work early anyway?"

"We just wrapped up early, so I thought I would come and surprise you." Her face quickly changed from puzzled to a painfully agitated expression. From that second I had a feeling the evening was plummeting downhill at an alarming rate.

I wonder if Harrison is having this much fun.

"If I'd known that you would have been out getting drunk with Harrison, I wouldn't have fucking bothered!"

She seemed somewhat disappointed with my choice of how to spend my day.

Surely, a guy can have a beer with his old pal from university, right?

"So, what you're saying is that you're upset that I went out with Harrison. Someone who I've known forever and has always been there for me, who *needed* me to be there for him!? Why don't you tell me what's really bugging you, Lisa? Because I know that it can't be that."

That's just bullshit.

"I'm not even going to entertain that," I continued. "Not for a second."

"It's the move, Joe."

I knew it, Lisa. I fucking knew it.

She wants to bail on me now just a few weeks from completion, doesn't she? Why did I bother looking at all those flats? Why did I settle on one that makes her life easier as opposed to being selfish and, heaven forbid, choosing one that might actually make me happy? Instead, I made a compromise, for her.

"What about the move, Lisa? We only have a few weeks left now, and we can be in there! Out of this place and into our very own pad."

"That's what I mean, Joe. I don't think I can do this."

"Do what, Lisa? Move in with me?"

I gazed upon her, and the look in her eye was really worrying. I couldn't tell if she wanted to cry, scream, or just run for the hills.

"Yeah Joe, it's so much to commit to."

"I don't get you, Lise. You've been super excited about the move, and now your expression looks as if the damn sky is falling."

"I know, Joe, and I was, but after today it just reminds me of how selfish you can be sometimes."

Selfish?

She has to be kidding me, right?

"I'm scared, Joe."

I had a feeling Lisa would be a little apprehensive about the move, but never that she'd freak out like this. She never got agitated before over a few dishes not washed in the flat before. Or a half empty beer can on the table.

I didn't like to see her sad. Hopefully, I could put her mind at ease so she could sleep soundly in the knowledge that I love her, and that I would do anything to make this work.

"I'm worried that this is going to fail Joe – it's such a big step."

"It is a big step, Lisa. You're right. But it's a step we're taking together and I wanna be there with you when it happens. It might be difficult, sure. But it's never easy making a huge adjustment in your life like this. Relationships are difficult enough these days and living together can sometimes complicate things even more, but without taking that plunge, how will we ever find out?

"Who knows? You might end up driving me mad in a month, or I you. Or it could be the best thing we've ever done.

"If we don't do this, you'll have to continue to stare at my hideous curtains, which you love so much. Either that or the world can see me strutting my stuff around the flat the way baby Jesus made me."

"That is true: those bloody curtains are *not* coming with us, Joe."

"Well Lisa, you'll have to pick some new ones out then, won't you?"

"I guess I'll have to. Hey, come here."

I took her hands and held them tight and looked deep into her eyes, and pulled her towards me.

"Look, Lisa, I'm not going to promise you that it will be a fairy-tale each day, and it wouldn't be fair to assume that it will be, but I promise you this: I fucking love you."

"I love you too, Joe."

"Shut up and kiss me."

I grabbed her by the ass and carried her into the bedroom and threw her onto the bed, heels and all. *Damn, she looks hot*, I thought. Even though it was only an old dress, to me she was perfect.

"Did you miss me then, Joe?"

Always baby.

She moaned as I rolled her onto her front and pushed her dress up so I could see that cute little behind of hers. I gave it a nice hard slap so it left a nice mark on her cheek.

"Am I branded with your hand now?"

"Damn right you are. I gotta show my dominance, right?"

I slowly slid the dress over her head and tossed it on the floor, leaving nothing but her black heels, and her underwear. She ripped my clothes off like an animal and we made love until we both fell asleep.

Morning was coming soon, a little slower than Lisa but, nevertheless, it was on its way.

The light began to beam through the awful curtains. *It looked like it could be a good day*, I thought as I rubbed the sleep from my eyes. She looked so peaceful sleeping there, all still and innocent.

Lisa began to stir.

"Morning beautiful."

"So would you like to talk about the move again? Or shall we go for round two? Then I'll take you to breakfast, before we have to head to work."

"I know what I'd like to eat, Joe."

"Round two then?" I replied. "Sounds good to me, Lisa, you can go on top this time. You look a little more graceful than I do. Especially your boobs, they're much nicer to look at than mine."

"Ah, don't feel bad, Joey! They could be a lot worse. Ha!"

"Thanks Lise, I know I can always count on you to say the right thing. I guess that's why I love you."

"You'd better, Joe. I don't want you running off into the sunset with Harrison now do I!?"

"Not a chance. You're stuck with me, I'm afraid."

"I wouldn't have it any other way, Joe."

***

"Thank fuck for that," I sighed as I arrived at the door from meeting with Joe. Home at last. I noticed that there was a light on whilst fumbling around for my keys in anticipation. This should be interesting...

HAPPY FUCKING MONDAY

always admired Lisa and Joe. For the most part, they were a pretty perfect couple, which almost sounds too good to be true. But they really were.

They rarely disagreed on anything and were near enough inseparable. They both worked very hard, and were both well-educated, Lisa especially – she was the editor for the top fashion magazine *Be Yourself,* and we all know what Joe does.

She was about 5'4" with blonde hair and she was a gorgeous little size 12. Even though she worked for a fashion magazine, she was never one to obsess over that kind of thing outside of her office. She was not one for vanity or being in a relationship with her own reflection. I'd always admired that about her. She was always one to do her own thing, and never one to follow the herd, which made her perfect for Joe. That was always a huge selling point for him, never one to want to control him, or he her, they always knew their own boundaries with minimal disagreements.

Joe was 5'10" with incredibly thick and dark brown hair and a pretty rocking dad bod.

Lisa was nothing like his ex-girlfriend.

Joe used to always open the car door for Jennifer and move the chair for her whenever they would go to dinner, acting real chivalrous, and she constantly threw it in his face. She never gave a damn about any of that, and never really appreciated any of those gestures, and expected him to do everything for her without giving anything in return.

I hope he made it back ok last night, and wasn't as drowned as I am. I really hope they can reach some common ground too and begin to finalise their plans for the move – unless, of course, there was another reason why she might be reluctant to continue with the commitment.

I took my keys out and, just as I reached for the door to get in, my phone rang. It's probably a good thing I'd passed out drunk in the stairwell by my door.

"*Harrison, it's Lisa.*"

"Everything ok, Lise? What's up?"

"Not really, Harrison, can we meet? Joe's in the shower so I need to be quiet."

"Sure, where's good for you?"

"Columbia's coffee shop, by the river – 9:30?"

"Sure."

"Ok, see you then."

"Bye."

At least I was dry, but being out all night, I was a little tired; I probably shouldn't have hit those other bars after Joe and I had left the Loch. I was pretty much ready to crawl right into my bed and call in sick.

As fragile as I was, I thought it best to hear Lisa out and make sure everything was ok with her and Joe. I just hoped that she hadn't done anything stupid. Even she had her moments sometimes, and she had a habit of getting herself into trouble, kind of like someone else I knew. Not to the same extent though. She just had a bad habit of speaking out of turn at times and mistiming her words. I guess that happens to everyone at some point though – especially yours truly. I've been guilty of that on more than one occasion.

I made it to Columbia's and grabbed a table by the window. Lisa was late. Punctuality was never her strong point.

Then Lisa walked in with an expression as grey as the weather. We ordered our drinks and began to talk.

"So what's on your mind, Lise?" I asked.

"I'm not quite sure how to say it really, Harrison."

"You can tell me anything. It can't be that bad, right?"

"I'm pregnant, Harrison. Well, there you go, I said that out loud."

"Yeah, Lisa you did." I paused. "Well, I thought you were going to tell me that you'd slept with five

44

of Joe's friends and then killed his mum, but that's not so bad."

"That's not funny, Harrison; I would never cheat on Joe, you know that, and I hope that he does too. It's also a pretty shitty analogy."

"Relax Lisa, I know that. So what are you so worried about? And why are you sitting here telling me and not Joe?"

"The truth is, I have no idea how to tell him. I'm worried that he'll freak out and just leave me! Last night, we were fighting after he came home from being out with you and I used the move as a scapegoat, like some stupid little teenager without the balls to say what's really on my mind."

"So what happened after you guys finished fighting? Did you manage to talk to him?"

"No, we ended up in bed, until the early hours of the morning."

"For Christ's sake, Lise."

"Well, it's not as if I can get pregnant twice, right?"

"That's not the point. You've got to tell him, I'm pretty sure he'll notice something is up when you start throwing up every morning. Not to mention the fact that stomach of yours is going to tell a story of its own before long, and I'm sure that may lead to a question, or two."

"Don't you think I know all of this, Joe?"

"I don't know, Lisa, do you? What are you really worried about? Tell me. I want you guys to be happy, you are my closest friends, and I only want the very best for you both. Also, you need to know that what you're both getting into is what you both *really* want. Moving into a flat is one thing, but a baby comes with a long and expensive contract… one not to be entered into flippantly. You know I will always be there for you guys, and I will back you all the way with whatever I can, but you don't need to do this one on your own, Lise. Besides, Joe loves the shit out of you. He would never bail on anything. I know him too well, and so should you, by now. You mean everything to him. The way he talks about you, you don't need to worry."

"Thanks Harrison. That means a lot to me. I think you're right too."

"Of course I'm right, Lisa. Trust me. If he does try to run though, I'll kick his ass for being a fucking hypocrite, and a quitter. Worse than that, he'll end up making me look bad, and I can't afford to let that happen, not now, not ever.

"Some people are afraid of commitment, Lisa, but if you're truly in this together then you can share the load. You both love each other, so it shouldn't have to be work, raising a child together can be the most beautiful gift for you both. Plus, it will be a great excuse to get me out of the flat, and away from Lilly, when I come to see you."

"Aw, are you two not getting along lately then, Harrison?"

"Not really. We had a bit of a bust up the other night, not sure if Joe mentioned. It was horrific, from what I can just about recall."

Yes, and the stairwell by my door is surprisingly comfortable.

"I guess you could say that I've pretty much drunk myself through my hangover but, now that I'm sober again, I can't remember a thing. I'm certain it's gonna hit me hard and fast soon enough, once I get back to the flat. Either that or Lilly is waiting for me with an axe – think *The Shining*, only with more terror."

Only time will tell.

"Well, let's hope not, for my sake at least."

"Why's that, Lise?"

"Well, Joe would probably be wanting a best man at some stage; if he ever proposes to me, I'm sure he would be honoured if you'd play the part."

"Lisa, I would love to, and I will be sure to expose all of your dirty little secrets. You never know though, he may still try and run away when you tell him the news!"

"So not funny, Harrison."

"Kidding! Everything will be fine, Lisa. I'm only playing with you."

"Shouldn't you head back? Lilly would probably have packed all of your shit in boxes (or hers) by now, wouldn't she?"

"Yeah, it's not something I can rule out at this stage. I should check on the flat and see if there's going to be any of my deposit left for me to collect too. Most of it looks like it'll go on the wall though, so we'll see, I suppose."

In my mind, I was playing out a million and one different scenarios, ranging from bags packed, to a nice angry letter, maybe even a voodoo doll with my head on it? (Or Off.)

"Who knows what's been going on while I've been on my little weekend bender?" I said. "You know *nothing* would surprise me, Lise. I fear the way she was acting up. So, what are you going to do tonight after work?"

"Go home, eat."

"After that?"

"Talk to Joe, right?"

"Exactly, and what are you going to talk about with Joe?"

"The little person growing inside of me."

"Damn right!" I said. "Please let me know how it goes, won't you? I'd love to be there to see the reaction on his face, but I'll most likely be busy dealing with my own reaction. I imagine it won't be terribly dissimilar from Edvard Munch's 'The Scream.'"

"Yeah, you do that, and text us if you need anything, won't you?"

"Thanks Lise, I will. And same to you guys."

I really do hope he takes that news well. I know he loves her but it's very dramatic, especially on a Monday morning after the weekend we've had.

Can't believe it, a little mini-Joe, or Lisa.

Exciting stuff.

I knew I should probably make a move: adventure beckons! Or chaos, so to speak – either or. "Ok Lise, shall we go? You gotta head to work, right?"

"Yeah. Not sure how I'm going to make it through, but I'll find a way."

"You'll be fine, just give me a call if you wanna talk. And don't worry about Joe; together you'll both build something beautiful."

"Thanks Harrison, that's so sweet of you to say."

"Well, I meant it. Lise, you guys are great together, and the new flat sounds amazing too. I'll come and help you move too, if my car hasn't been set alight."

"Ha ha, you're on."

"Let's rock."

What the fuck am I doing?

Do I really want to go back to the flat? Do I *need* to go back? I can shower at the university, right? And then I could just buy new clothes and things like that.

No, I gotta face the music.

Just as I was leaving Columbia's, I heard a voice that made my blood run cold. It was Tammy, one of Lilly's friends. *How the hell did we not notice her sat there?*

"Hey dickhead, what have you done to upset Lilly? She called me last night in tears saying you two had a huge row over your usual bullshit."

Now Tammy and I did not get on at the best of times. Somehow, I had the feeling that today would not be any different.

She was about 5' 7" with wiry blonde hair and she was super skinny, kind of like a skeleton wandering about the place, tormenting the living with her ghastly-looking teeth. She had abnormally large hands too. I mean, fucking massive.

It was the stuff of nightmares, really.

Luckily, Lisa had swiftly made her escape and didn't have to endure the wrath that was Tammy's resting bitch face and, not to mention, her camel-flavoured breath. She and Lilly had been friends for a long time, from way before I met her, but somehow she had always felt wronged in some way. Almost as if, with me in the picture, I had stolen her friend and taken a piece of her away, not that I had ever made any ploy to try and keep them apart.

Lilly is a big girl and she can see whoever she likes. I'd never made an effort to stop her hanging out with any of her friends, past or present.

Why the fuck did she have to bump into me on today of all days?

"Well, Tammy, it sounds as though you've answered your own question there, doesn't it?"

"Don't get smart with me, Harrison. I'm not an idiot, you know!"

"Could have fooled me."

"What was that, prick!?" I can see her getting angrier by the second.

"Nothing, Tammy."

The hostess came over, looking a little upset; and some of the other customers had stopped sipping their mocha lattes to watch and listen in on what was going on; this was probably the most excitement they'd seen on a Monday morning in a long time.

"Could you please keep it down or take it outside? Columbia's is a family café." The hostess looked panicked and very uneasy as she made her request.

"I'm sorry, miss. I apologise for my friend. She's a little cranky this morning and she hasn't eaten breakfast yet. We were just leaving."

"I'm not his friend; he's a bloody idiot, and a womaniser!"

"Bit of a fallacy, if you ask me, but not to worry." I watched her fume at that. "I'm sorry, Tammy," I added, "please carry on, I actually have all day. It's not as if I have to get to work or anything like that. My students will have to take care of themselves for a few minutes without me."

"What the hell were you doing here with her anyway? You should be back home with Lilly trying to sort your shit out!"

"Well, we were having coffee, obviously, not that it's any of your business," I replied. "Satisfied?"

"NO, Harrison, far from it. Why do you always have to be so sarcastic?"

"Why do you always have to be a fucking bitch?"

"Don't call me a bitch!" she snapped.

"Well, prove me wrong, Tammy."

"I don't have to prove nothing to you, Harrison. It's because I think you're a wanker and I don't like you."

"We'll nobody's forcing you to talk to me, Tammy. Also, this is a coffee shop. If you don't like it, you are free to leave whenever you like."

"What do you mean 'just having coffee'?"

"It's a coffee shop," I replied. "Isn't it?"

"Don't be sarcy with me, you little dickhead!"

"Whatever you say, Tammy. You're the boss. Besides, it's none of your damn business who I drink coffee with, or anyone else's for that matter."

"Don't patronise me either, Harrison," Tammy said. "I'm about to call Lilly and tell her to tell you to go fuck yourself!"

Oh lovely. I began to wonder if I may be able to solve all of my problems in one hit. Get rid of Lilly, have a nice clean flat.

But it was an interesting take on the situation; she's cleverer than she looks, I think. I mean, I get that she's looking out for her friend. But that's just Tammy, I suppose.

"Lilly is just so perfect, right, Tammy, there's no way she could do any wrong at all, is there?"

"Well no, Harrison, even women are at fault at times."

"*Really?* Shit, I had no idea!" I replied. "Thanks a lot, Confucius, I feel so enlightened now. I honestly hadn't really thought about it that way. You know, all this time I've been blaming myself for every little thing that goes wrong!"

"Really, Harrison?"

"No, Tammy not now, not ever."

So fucking what? I can always admit when I'm wrong, which is so much more than can be said for most of the people I know. The way that I see it is quite simple really: if you don't even bother to try, then you have already failed. It's that simple. I've never failed or quit on anything. If it goes south with Lilly, then so what? Life will go on; but not until I've given it my everything. Then I can say that I tried.

I smiled casually and left. "Lovely to see you, as always."

"Piss off."

She gave me the finger as I walked away.

Charming.

That lovely little reunion had cost me a lot of precious time. I was not gonna have time to shower and change.

What a beautiful day it's turning out to be. I really hope the fucking tube is running; I really can't afford to be late today.

I had so much to do at work it was unreal. Papers to mark, lectures to write.

Not to mention, a class in forty minutes.

Fuck.

LOOK JOE, BLUE

"Joe, try and escape work early tonight, if you can. I have news!"

"Ooh, ok I'll try," I replied. "Anything exciting, Lise?"

"I think so, yeah."

"Alright hun, I'll see you tonight. I'll let you know when I'm on my way back."

***

After a packed train ride, I finally made it to class, only a few minutes late. Just as well too, half of my students were missing. *Well done, Harrison.*

Maybe they were hungover too.

Work was going well that morning, considering how poorly my day began. The classes were great and the kids that bothered to turn up were paying attention.

Heading back to the flat would be fun; who knows what awaited me? I should probably have checked my phone to see if there was anything from Lilly. Just as I was packing up, I heard a knock on my door; it was Mike, my boss.

What the fuck does he want? Can't he see I wanna get the hell out of here?

"Harrison, how are you doing? Good day?" Mike asked, with a somewhat suspicious look about him.

"Hey Mike. Err, yeah, not too bad. How are you doing? What can I do for you this fine afternoon?"

"Well, Harrison, I wanted to wait and do this on Friday, but I think we can get it over with now really. Have you got a minute?"

Shit, this can't be good. Is Mike planning to despatch with me too? I haven't slept with any students. I don't do that anymore; it's mainly a sausage fest here anyway.

"Sure thing, Mike, what's up?"

"Well, I wanted to talk to you about Jack."

"Sure, what about him?" I asked.

"He's leaving, as of this week."

"Really, Mike, how come? He's been here forever!"

"That's the problem, Harrison. We need some fresh perspective on this place, plus he was fiddling the accounts with that bitch Sue from finance."

Well, I only hope he wasn't fiddling Sue too.

"So, what's the plan for replacing him then?" I asked.

"Well, Harrison, you've been here for a while now, haven't you?"

"Yeah, six years next month, Mike."

"Exactly, you've been with us a while and you're the best guy we've had in this hell hole, nobody knows their stuff better than you, and you've earned it."

"Wow, can I think about it?"

"What's there to think about?" he asked. "You'll get your own office, and an extra 10k in your wallet too."

"Sold, Mike!"

"Brilliant. I'll get HR to draw up the contracts this afternoon."

"Thanks Mike. I really appreciate that."

"A word of advice though, my boy," he said. "Don't fuck up, and don't fuck Sue either! I'm just kidding, she's gone too. If you know any people that can operate an abacus, you send me their CV across. I don't care if they have three eyes, I'll take them."

"Will do, Mike."

"Oh, and Harrison, is your shower broken? You look like crap."

"On it! Thanks again. Mike, have a good evening."

I took a quick glance at my phone as I was making my escape from the office. No missed calls, nothing. Although I can't say I'm surprised.

Well, today was a fucking good day. Let's see if I can't keep this momentum going.

I made it home, dry this time, and the lift was fixed too – bonus. Once I'd made my way up to the door, I finally got in. And, what do you know? The flat was empty; not even a note. Nothing. The place looked the same as it did when I had left it, although a little part of me wasn't surprised; I guess I was expecting more, or less, depending on how you look at it, at the very least. A set of new locks on the door, maybe. I suppose I should probably clean up before I end up in need of a tetanus jab, with all that glass on the floor…

At least I'll have the double to myself tonight. I can starfish – amazing! I'm surprised she hasn't texted me though. I should give her a text to see if she's alright.

Whilst cleaning, I heard my phone go. It was probably Joe. *I wonder if Lisa has shared her news.* I felt almost glad when I saw her name on there. It was Lilly. I opened the message.

"Fuck you. Don't text me again."

Right, then. Where's the hoover?

The flat was looking cleaner, so that was nice.

Maybe I'll leave her to it; it's possible she's still mad at me. I'll probably end up doing more harm than good at this stage.

Just as I was finishing up with the cleaning, I heard a knock at the door.

Now, I wonder who that could be? God, I just hope it isn't Sue really.

"Joe, how are you doing? Come in, man!" I could tell by the look on his face that he had something on his mind. Had Lisa dropped the news about the baby?

"So what's on your mind, buddy? Bit late for you, isn't it?"

"I suppose it is actually, yeah," he replied. "The flat looks good, though. Finally got around to cleaning it then."

"Yeah man. Just about. Bloody busy day but very productive too!"

"I see that you still have Edvard's masterpiece on the wall over there?"

"Yeah," I said. "Well, I think it adds character to the place, y'know? Perhaps I'll keep it."

"Any word from the talented artist at all?"

"Briefly," I replied. "She was, hmm… how can I put this delicately? Very much still pissed at me."

"Say no more."

"So how is Joe on this wonderful Monday evening? Has one of your buildings collapsed? You know that I can't be an accessory to your crimes, right?"

"Nah, nothing like that," he said. "Well, not that I'm aware of."

"You got the spare passports and cash, right?"

"Sure."

"I'm good, though," I said. "Really, work is great and all."

He didn't seem to hear me. "Lisa is playing on my mind though," he said, "as always. She said she wants to '*talk*'."

"So, what's so bad about that?" I asked. "Wanna drink, man?"

"Sure."

As I handed him the beer, I could tell that the anxiety was eating away at him. It killed me knowing the news before him, but I had to keep quiet, for both their sakes, it wasn't my place to say.

"Thanks Harrison."

"Relax, man," I said. "I'm sure everything is fine. Have you tried talking to Lise at all?"

"No. I'm gonna talk to her tonight. She's probably pissed at me too; I told her I would try and leave work early, if I could."

"Well, you don't know what it is," I said. "It could be anything. Try not to read too much into it. No point worrying about something that you can't control. Life's too short to stress over things like that, you know? You should probably get back to her soon though. It's getting kinda late."

"Yeah, you're probably right!"

"Now go on, get the fuck out of here, Joe. Go home to that beautiful girl."

"Thanks for the beer, man. Catch you soon."

"Alright pussy. Text me if you need anything."

"You too, Harrison."

I almost felt as if I was betraying him a little, but it was a very difficult position to be in – the fact it was Lisa that told me first. I hope he will handle it well, although nothing can ever truly prepare you for something like this. Especially if it's a surprise to both of you. I just hope he reacts in the right way, otherwise he'll probably be kicked out too.

A homeless architect, oh the irony.

I suppose he can build a new house, worst-case scenario. I thought I might celebrate the newly cleansed flat with a beer, but after checking the fridge, I realised it was empty.

The horror.

Next stop, the corner shop. I just got promoted, so I figured I would treat myself.

Now I had beer and a clean flat, so I grabbed myself some food and relaxed for a fresh start in the morning, looking forward to getting into that new office! Happiness arrived in the form of a takeaway delivery man – much nicer than having to clean the kitchen, again.

Just as I was heading to bed, I could hear footsteps outside in the corridor. I had this strange feeling in the pit of my stomach that my perfect Monday was about to come unstuck.

Suddenly, I heard a loud banging on the door – someone was really hammering away at it, like they were the damn police! I peeked through the spyhole.

It was Mary, my ex.

What the hell does she want!?

I opened the door and, before I knew it, I nearly lost an eye on the coat hook. She'd slapped me, hard.

"That's for not texting me back, dickhead!"

"Excuse me, Mary?"

"The last time we'd spoken, Harrison, I told you that I might be carrying your child, and you didn't bother to fucking reply to my message. How insensitive can one person be?"

"Well, Mary, I was most likely in shock at how you chose to deliver that bombshell, and it's not like I didn't try to call you. So are you going to tell me what happened? Are you here to collect some money from me?"

"No," she replied. "Actually, it was a false alarm in the end, so you're off the hook… for now."

"Thanks, I guess. That's kind of you," I said. "Wait a minute. I'm starting to remember this now; I must have tried to block it out. We spoke about this after you faked the fucking pregnancy test, remember? And you tried to trap me!?"

"Oh, don't be so melodramatic, Harrison."

"That's a bit of an understatement, don't you think, Mary? You can't screw with people's lives like that. That's just messed up!"

I could tell by the look in her eyes that she couldn't care less.

"Why?" she asked. "People do it all the time. You hear stories every other week about stuff like that."

"Jesus Christ, Mary," I snapped. "You literally don't give a shit, do you?"

"Well, you're safe, so don't panic."

"Do you want to tell me what you want?"

"Just this…"

She grabbed my balls and pushed me up against the wall and kissed me. While trying to rip my shirt off and drag me into the bedroom, she somehow still managed to get her own top off and tossed it aside. All the time, she never lost sight of her goal: undress me as quickly as she could.

"Mary, what are you doing? I'm with someone right now."

I gently tried to push her away from me without hurting her, knowing how headstrong she could be when she set her mind to something.

"I really want you back, Harrison. I want to feel every inch of that body."

"Sorry Mary, I can't," I replied. "My relationship has already become a bit of a minefield lately as it is. I just can't afford to step on another one right now."

"What's the matter?" she asked. "Don't you find me attractive anymore?"

"I never stopped finding you attractive, Mary. That was never the problem. We always had our issues, but none of them extended to the bedroom, from what I can remember."

"You're right, that was one area where we always worked," she replied. "We just screwed up everything else… I love you, Harrison."

"Really?" I asked. "I never got that vibe in the time that we were together. Now, I'm not trying to be a dick, but that's what I felt. I can't go back to that, Mary. I think we were just too toxic as a couple, you know?"

Tempted as I was though – and I mean, don't get me wrong, Mary was still hot as hell, not to mention, highly persuasive – I was in enough shit as it was with Lilly. Even though I didn't know how this thing was going to work out, if at all, Lilly and I were still together, and I had to stay true to that.

"Goodnight Mary."

Damn, where the hell are my cigarettes?

That was intense. Although, as much as that would have been a great end to my day, I can't start another fire before I've extinguished the first one. I needed another drink after that. I could hear my phone going off; seriously, what do all these people want with me on a Monday night, for Christ's sake? All I wanted to do was relax and try to get an early night.

"Hey Joe, what's up?"

"Harrison, I think something's happened to Lisa. I can see her through the window, but she's on the floor not moving! I can't find my keys either. Can you have a look around to see if I left them at yours, please – and hurry!"

"Joe, I've found them. I'll be right over."

"Thanks Harrison. Try and be as quick as you can, buddy. I'm freaking out over here!"

"Of course. I'm heading to the car now."

Damn, I really hope Lisa is ok, and the baby! I could feel my body full of adrenaline as I ran to the car. I don't know how the hell Joe would go on without her, let alone the baby.

***

"Joe, I'm outside, coming up now."

As we rushed, opening the door and running inside, I prayed to God that mother and child were both ok.

"LISA! Wake up!" We started to gently shake her. She was breathing. Joe let out a sigh of relief as she showed signs of movement and slowly awoke.

"What happened to you? You scared the shit out of me, woman!"

"Sorry, Joe, I don't know," she replied. "I guess I must have passed out."

"Clearly, but in the middle of the kitchen?" Joe said. "Have you taken something?"

"Taken something, Joe?"

"Yes."

"I'm not on any drugs," she said, "if that's what you mean, Joe."

"Ok, so what is it?"

"Well, I've been feeling pretty weak lately and easily agitated."

"Lisa, come on now," I said. "You gotta be straight with him; he's been tearing his hair out for a few hours now."

"What is it, Lise? What the hell are you not telling me?"

"Harrison?" Joe looked at me, puzzled.

"It's best you hear it from Lisa, Joe," I said.

"I was going to tell you tonight, Joe."

"Tell me what, Lisa?"

"I'm pregnant."

"And you told Harrison first?" Joe looked us both up and down and let out a sigh, although he seemed more relieved that she was ok, above anything else.

"Only because I thought you would freak out, Joe. I was worried you would run a mile, and I know that you trust Harrison as he's known you forever, I just didn't know how to handle it."

"Harrison, can you call an ambulance for us please?"

"Sure thing, man."

"Why would I need an ambulance?" she asked. "I'm ok."

"Lisa, don't argue with me," Joe snapped. "You may be ok, but I want them to get you checked out, even if it means carrying you there myself!"

"Yes, sir."

"Why on earth would I freak out?" Joe asked suddenly. "I love you. Do you really think that I would skip town? Come on, Lisa, you gotta give me some credit. We're building something pretty stable here right now, especially with the new move. We'll need a bigger place, and a baby cage, so little Logan can't escape at night."

"I don't know," she said. "I guess my hormones are running away with me right now, Joe."

"I'll say, they've got to be to think that I would ever do something like that. You know we're moving in together soon, right? I think I might pick up on that at some point, you know? Especially if you end up throwing up each morning. Not to mention, that cute little midriff of yours might expand a little bit."

"I know," she said. "I'm sorry."

"I can't wait to have a little mini-me running around the place!"

"Who said it's going to be a boy, Joe? I haven't even had my first scan yet! It could be a girl."

"Ok, well, if it's a girl she'll be little Clara," he said. "And, if it is, she will be incredible; full of charm, charisma and talent, and if she's anything like her mum, I guess she won't be too harsh on the eyes either."

"Ambulance will be here in ten minutes guys," I said.

"Thanks Harrison."

I think, at that moment, while they were talking, I could tell that everything was going to be fine. The way they looked at each other, at that moment, their whole life changed.

"Clara and Logan, hmm," she said. "We can always circle back to that one I think, Joe."

"I guess I can forgive you, Lisa," he replied, "but I'm going to miss that muffin top of yours. Come over here – let's get you on to the sofa while we wait for the paramedics." Then he turned to me. "You can head back now, Harrison, if you want?"

"You sure, Joe?" I asked. "Are you two going to be alright? I don't mind hanging around for you."

"Sure man, we'll be ok. Thank you again."

"No problem, you two. Make sure that you take care of her, and go easy on him, Lise. Logan is a badass name, and Clara too. Let me know if anything changes, ok? See you guys soon."

Well, that was not my average Monday. Never a dull moment with those two around, I think, and then there was me somehow caught in the midst of the chaos.

***

I heard from Joe in the morning; they'd kept her overnight, just to be on the safe side. Both Mum and Baby were perfectly healthy. Fantastic news, and a huge weight lifted from everyone's mind! All they asked at the hospital was that she relaxed a little bit.

I hope they look out for each other. They'll need all the rest they can get; it's going to be a long road ahead. And I can't wait to meet little Logan or Clara.

Excitement!

THE GIRL FROM THE CAFÉ

Back at work, things were pretty damn sweet. I'd just signed my contract to take over the job, and more importantly, from a hedonistic point of view, I was looking forward to setting foot in that shiny new office. Mike was happy, and I was kicking ass with the students.

I'd also heard from Joe; both Mum and Baby were doing great. Awesome news – I really couldn't wait to meet the little person once they arrived.

Still no word from Lilly, either, she must really be pissed at me. Naturally, I'd recovered from my hangover, but still couldn't quite piece together what might have ticked her off so much. I was sure it would come back to me though, and when I least expected it.

I made my way over to Jay's to grab a bite after work and ordered the usual beer. Then I sat outside by the water; I figured I would try and make the most of the weather while it lasted. The place was bustling for a weeknight, which was quite surprising as there were no bands on that night, but there were still some great vibes.

As I sat down, I could hear random screaming and a suspect-looking guy heading my way.

There goes my evening. Fantastic.

The guy looked like a real tweaker, unable to stand still and twitching constantly. He was asking people for money outside the bar, but nobody was biting. For a moment, I thought it might have been Craig in some poor attempt to bait me into causing more trouble for myself and starting something. Finally, the guy moved on; maybe he'd get his fix from around the other side of town – anywhere but here, while I'm enjoying my pint.

As I casually sipped my second beer, a familiar face was heading my way, but I couldn't figure out where from. Whoever she was, she looked incredible, and rather punk rock-like, with black knee-high boots, a short dress that sat high above her knees, and a kind of Grim Reaper-style tattoo, covering most of her leg. She came and sat down next to me on the empty table.

"Hey, trouble."

She smiled and looked me up and down.

"You're cute. So, where's your buddy tonight?"

It was the hostess from the Benedict looking very different, so much so that I didn't even recognise her.

"He's at home, I hope, looking after his very recently pregnant girlfriend. So it's just me tonight, I'm afraid."

"Ah, ok. So, what about you? Is there a lucky lady in your life? Someone waiting to ask where you've been when you get back from a night out? Hoovering while you nurse your hangover?"

Sarcasm, and a cheeky look about her, I like this one.

"There is not, sadly no. She's probably cursing me to all her friends right now."

"So, you two are getting on well then?" she asked. "Have you been together long?"

"Well, we did for a while, but we've not spoken since the other day when I saw you for breakfast. Sounds very illicit, doesn't it? 'When I saw you for breakfast'?"

"Cheeky."

"So what do they call you?" I asked.

"Charlotte, mostly."

"Well, it's very nice to meet you, Charlotte," I said. "I'm Harrison. Would you like to join me?"

She made her way over to my table, while in my head I weighed up the pros and cons of staying out with her.

"My girlfriends are all being pretty boring, y'know? They're not always a fan of the whole weekday drinking thing."

"Fucking amateurs."

"I know, right!"

"What about you?" I asked. "No boyfriend?"

"Smooth, Mr Hangover, very smooth. But aren't you in enough trouble?"

"I probably am. Hmm, I should probably make a move soon, Charlotte."

"Oh, really, that's a shame. Especially when I don't have a boyfriend."

"Well, I guess I could stick around for a little while, for my favourite hostess."

"Aw, that's sweet of you to say."

This girl is crazy beautiful. I'm rather surprised that she is on her own, especially with that razor-sharp wit. And that hair. After a while I could see myself getting a little too comfortable and, as much as I'd loved to have stayed, I made tracks to leave.

"Great to see you again, Charlotte. I'm sure I'll be hungover again at some stage."

"You too, Harrison."

"See you at breakfast."

"I look forward to it."

***

Once I'd arrived back at the flat, I could hear faint noises inside. As I was searching for my keys, I could sense that feeling in my stomach again.

As I opened the door, the last thing I could remember was feeling a massive blow to the back of my head, and then darkness.

***

I awoke slowly to find myself tied up in the kitchen. I could hear murmured voices, coming from the other room. The voices were getting more aggressive as they made their way towards me.

"I want you to pack up your fucking shit and leave Lilly the fuck alone. DO YOU HEAR ME? You're gonna leave town and stay the fuck away from her, understand?"

Who the fuck was this guy? And why was the other one standing there saying nothing?

I'd like to think that he was maybe the brains of the operation, but it hardly takes a huge amount of innovation to knock someone out when they don't even see you coming.

Am I crazy? Do I think too logically?

"Why wouldn't I wanna do that? Who the fuck are you, anyway?"

All of a sudden, I felt the cold steel edge of what felt like a machete pressed against my neck.

"What are you planning to do with that? Make me a sandwich?"

All of this talking was getting tiresome.

Either do something or get the fuck out of here so I can grab another beer before I crash out for the night.

"Why don't you two kids take your masks off?" I asked. "Obviously your balls must be pretty small, if you have to come with a knife, and your boyfriend over there. Does he hold your dick for you while you pee too?"

The one that was holding the knife wasn't doing the talking, which I thought was a little strange.

What the hell is this, amateur hour?

"Who we are doesn't matter, dickhead. Just do what we say, listen carefully, and that'll be the end of it."

Why the hell would I want to leave town? Things are going really well right now, all things considered.

"So, what happens if I stay? Are you going to kill me in my kitchen? I've only just replaced this flooring, you know."

Whilst the blade was pressed up against my throat, I wondered how sincere he actually was; well, the one talking anyway. The other one just stood there, just a poor excuse for a "yes man", dancing for some deranged puppet master. There could really only be one person responsible for this, and I had a pretty good idea of who.

"What do you think, fuck face?"

"Well, I'm not sure. Who's the giver and who's the receiver out of you two?" I sarcastically asked them.

"What the fuck is that supposed to mean, Harrison?"

"He's the dominant one, right? And you jump like his little bitch? Is that about the size of it? The least he can do is pay for the lube."

The little spoon – or the one that didn't speak, if you will – took the blade away and they went into another room and I could hear them arguing about what to do with me.

"We're getting the fuck out of here," one of them shouted. "Just remember what we said!"

I hopped over to the kitchen drawer in an attempt to grab a knife to cut myself loose, and fell on my ass, but as I was staring at the floor, I caught a glimpse of my freedom.

Thank God for open-plan living! I could see something shiny out of the corner of my eye, something poking out from under the sofa. It was a shard of glass from the smashed photo frame.

Apparently, I didn't do too good a job cleaning up the other day, and quite understandably so. I managed to cut myself free with minimal damage to my hands.

Cup of tea, and bed, then.

DESK MOVE

It was morning again, and here I was with another headache – not from the beer though this time, much to my liver's gratitude. However, it wasn't all headaches and sadness; I'd just got a text from Joe.

He and Lisa were on their way home!

The hospital had released her after she'd collapsed the other night. Naturally, that was enough to put a spring in my step. After all, it was really nice news to hear first thing.

"That's great, Joe. I'll be over later to say 'hi', if you're both feeling up to it. For now though, it's back on the grind with those pesky kids."

Once I'd arrived at the office, I noticed Mike had a bottle of champagne and a shiny new key in his hand. He was looking especially pleased with himself.

"Congratulations, buddy."

"What's going on, Mike?" I asked.

"I had them fit your office out overnight for you, Harrison."

"Ah Mike, you bloody legend. Thanks so much, man. I really can't tell you how much I appreciate it."

"Then don't. Just keep doing what you're doing," he said. "You earned this. Just remember to take stock of the good, and enjoy it."

"Thanks Mike. I think I can manage that."

"Join me for a glass then?" Mike said, producing a bottle of champagne from his desk drawer. It was a bit early, even for him.

"Sure, not the whole bottle though. You still have students today, don't you?"

"One class, yeah. Then I'll be balls deep in admin for the rest of the afternoon."

"Yeah, you and me both, brother."

We made our toast and carried on with our day.

"Thanks Mike. I'm not gonna let you down."

"I know you won't, Harrison."

Still no word from the elusive Lilly.

She must really be pissed at me.

It's not as if I'm not trying. I can't exactly head over there – I don't even know where she is.

I'm sure she will let me know when she's ready to talk. Hopefully not with a smoke signal coming from my flat, at least, but the old-fashioned way. Like… I don't know… a phone call maybe?

I found that I was able to hammer through my work a lot faster than I had hoped, today. Class was a breeze too; the kids were on their A-game, which made life a hell of a lot easier.

After work, I'd set off to see how Joe was getting on with Lisa. Hopefully he wouldn't be stressing too much now she was home, although I was sure she'd have him running around like a mad man. Quite rightly so too; he'll have to get used to that from the jump.

"Hey Harrison, how are you doing, man?"

"I'm great, buddy," I replied. "I had bit of a rough night though, but more on that later. On the plus side though, I moved into my new office this morning. Long live the king! How are you guys doing, and where's Mum?"

"Ah, she's sleeping right now, dude. She's had a rough few days, so she's keeping a low profile for now."

"That's good, Joe," I said. "She'll need her rest – do they know why she collapsed?"

"Yeah, the doctors said that she wasn't eating enough, or getting enough vitamins, so they've given us enough pills to open up a backstreet pharmacy."

"Make sure you feed her properly too, man. She'll need her strength, plus she's eating for two now. It's all on you, buddy, to take care of them."

"Always, man," Joe said. "She's in good hands."

I believed him too. Once he'd been given that news, I knew that he would have to pull himself together and be the best man he could be, for himself, and more importantly for his family.

"So, are you guys going to have a boy or a girl?"

"We're going to wait to find out, I think, unless Lisa changes her mind. In which case it will probably be decided for me."

Joe had a very different look in his eye. It was difficult to say if he was terrified or excited. Most likely both, I think.

"Ha, I hear you," I said. "You're going to have to get used to that, Joe."

"So what's up with you?" he asked. "You said you had a rough night…"

"Yeah, it was umm interesting, that's for sure. I was tied up and held at knifepoint in my kitchen."

"Fuck, Harrison. I'll say!"

"I know, right?"

"Do you have any idea who might be responsible for what happened?" he asked.

"Well, Joe, I have a few, but I'm not sure that I can prove anything right now. I'm sure it will all come to light sooner or later."

"How do you manage to get yourself mixed up in so much hassle and, more often than not, come out smelling like roses?"

"Ha, not sure about that, Joe. I do like to think of myself as both fireman and arsonist though."

"Yeah Harrison," he said. "I'd actually picked up on that." Then he paused for a moment. "Do you think it might have anything to do with Lilly? Or her brother, maybe?"

"I'm not sure, man. I just don't know right now," I replied. "One of them seemed a similar sort of build and height, but they didn't say much. The other one did all the talking."

"Well, that's not suspicious at all."

"Yeah, that's pretty much what I was thinking when it was going down."

"Hmm, well, have you heard anything from Lilly?" Joe asked. "Or is she still off the grid?"

"Not a word, nothing," I replied. "I did try to reach out to her today, actually, but I've not had anything back at all."

"Damn, what did you do, Harrison?"

"I don't really wanna go into it right now, man," I said. "You got enough to worry about without my shit too. I should probably be heading back in a minute. I suppose I should make some attempt to be fresh for my shiny new office."

"No worries," Joe said. "Let me know if you need anything, bro, and congratulations again on the job and the office!"

"Thanks Joe!"

As much as I would have loved to unload on Joe about my Lilly troubles, he had enough to worry about, so there was no need to add any extra weight to his mind.

Plus, he'd probably just lecture me and call me out on my bullshit, and who wants that?

He'll hear about it soon enough, I'm sure – most likely via the local news. I really couldn't stop myself from wondering about what had happened the previous night and would be lying if I'd told myself I wasn't a little shook up. Maybe it was a joint venture with another trashy individual who would remain nameless, for now.

Maybe I should go and confront Craig and his buddies, although I was not sure that was the best of ideas; he might not be the smartest, but he was probably already expecting that. Besides that, I don't really want to go looking for trouble. If he wants me, then he knows where to find me.

Leaving, though, was never going to be an option.

I wasn't about to be run out of town because of a couple of cowards, who didn't even make me a sandwich after all that time we spent together in the kitchen the other night.

There's only one other person I could think of that would be ballsy enough to act the way they did that night

Mary.

Was she upset that I wasn't prepared to spend the night with her? Did she create some awkward noise complaints while we were having our Late night domestic dispute?

Possible, but not likely.

Although something told me I hadn't seen the last of her.

I figured I would head over to the Final Final for a couple on my way home, see what was going on around that way, and maybe grab a bite too. I'd ordered my regular beer, and posted myself in my regular spot, where I could still people-watch, and catch up on the sports.

Like a true barfly.

As I peered around the room, I noticed a friendly face walking towards the bar, and I wondered if I should maybe go and say hello. There she was again. It was Charlotte.

Damn, this girl has something about her; just the way she carries herself makes me almost want to change everything about me. Screw it, I made my way over and asked if she would join me.

"Hey, handsome," she said. "What's a boy like you doing in a place like this?"

"Hey, Charlotte, how you doing?"

"Hey, Harrison, I'm great!" she replied. "How are things at home, handsome? I haven't seen you nursing a hangover in a while."

"Hmm, that's a hostile question, Charlotte."

"Well, good luck, anyway."

"So, how is the writing going?" I asked. "Or is it a secret?"

"I don't mind talking a little about it, as it's you."

"Aw, thanks Charlotte."

"It's a murder mystery, and I'm about a little over halfway through my first draft right now."

"That's incredible, Charlotte. Do you know how it ends just yet? Or are you still figuring it out?"

"Yeah, you know I'm playing with a few different ideas," she smiled as she replied. "I'm just deciding on the best one to go forward with, then I'll work towards it."

"Nice. Well, good luck, Charlotte," I said. "I'd love to have a read once it's finished."

Man, I'm getting increasingly more intrigued by the minute with this girl. I know that I probably shouldn't, but she's very interesting.

"Of course you can," she said. "I will give you a signed copy too, once it's out there."

"Thanks Charlotte, I'd really like that."

"So why aren't you over at Jay's tonight? Too cold for you?"

"Ha, cheeky. No, I just like this place. I gotta mix it up a bit, right? Can't be too much of a regular, propping up the same bar constantly."

"I feel you."

Damn, I wish you would.

Luckily for me, I hadn't given that too much thought otherwise something else might be craving attention; not that he has the decision-making authority around here.

"So, aren't you going to buy the lady a drink?" she asked, with a glint in her eyes.

"Sure, and what would Charlotte like?" I asked to satisfy her.

A few hours went by, *and drinks*, and I'll admit I was having fun. A part of me felt a little guilty for hanging out, and I wasn't even sure why.

Charlotte had a hell of a lot going for her: sass, brains, and the looks too. Not to mention the fact she was so easy to talk to.

A good listener is always someone you should pay attention to.

Lilly had all these things too, but maybe a little too much attitude at times, I think. Too much of that lately. I think we were getting to the point where we couldn't stand to be in the same room as each other. I really do hope that she reaches out, despite our bullshit. It would be nice to talk without the desire to tear each other's eyes out.

After a few more drinks, we were still talking. She had a cheeky look about her.

Suddenly, she leant in and kissed me.

"I'm sorry," she said. "I don't know what came over me. I think you're cute." She smiled with a sort of nervous yet pleased look about her.

"You don't need to apologise. I won't feel guilty though. As you kissed me, I can play the victim. Listen Charlotte, you're crazy beautiful, but I have too much going on right now and it just wouldn't be right."

"Oh, but Harrison, I only want a little nibble."

"There's nothing I would love more than to scratch that itch for you, Charlotte, but I think it would just get me into a whole world of pain. Even more than I'm already in, if you can believe that."

"I guess I will have to just get my vibrator out and think of you while I waste away those energiser bunnies."

Jesus, why would she talk to me like that?

"You're a bad influence on me, Charlotte. How is a boy meant to sleep at night with those kinds of images floating about in his head? I am gonna go now before I drag you back to my place."

I hugged her as I was leaving, and she grabbed my balls, nice and hard, but I was determined not to break, despite the booze.

"Goodnight trouble. Nice bulge by the way."

"Thanks, I grow it myself."

Just as I was leaving, I noticed a car out front of the bar that had been there from the moment I had arrived. As I was making my way home, the car began to speed up pretty quickly. I figured the guy was probably just drunk or something.

The last thing that I can remember was hearing three loud bangs.

They sounded like gunshots.

LIGHTS OUT

I suppose I had better get in touch with Mike and let him know the situation.

At this point I think I could be forgiven for letting my mind move a million miles a minute at the thought of who might have been responsible for what had just gone down outside the bar. At least the food wasn't the worst I've eaten, much better than my old school dinners.

Mike had dropped by to see me in the Intensive Care Unit.

"What the fuck happened to you!?"

"Well, Mike, I was shot leaving a bar last night."

"I'm glad you have your sense of humour about you, Harrison," he said. "That's good."

He had a pretty odd look in his eye, one I wasn't really used to. I was hoping it was relief though, for the sake of my promotion.

"What did the doctor say, Harrison?"

"They're happy with how the surgery went," I said. "Luckily both bullets that hit me missed anything critical, but they want to keep me in for a couple of days."

"Sure thing, Harrison. Well, don't rush on my account," he said. "Take all the time you need, won't you? I'll be sure to save your workload for when you come back."

"Thanks Mike, aren't you just the greatest?"

"I'm kidding, you crazy bastard. I won't let you come back to a mountain of bullshit after being shot twice. Just let me know when you're ready to come back."

"Cheers Mike, I appreciate that."

"Don't mention it," he said.

A few days later I was back to my normal dysfunctional self again, but a visit from Joe and Lisa was something I was looking forward to. Positive energy would be welcome right now.

That wasn't before a visit from some of the city's finest. They came to ask me a few questions about what had happened by the bar. I gave them as much as I could, but my head was so hazy and everything seemed to be moving so fast that it was impossible to take myself back there and think of something tangible to give them.

They said they would look into it.

"There he is," Joe shouted. "Trouble with a capital H!"

"Hey guys, how are you doing?"

"We're good," Lisa said. "You look like you've seen better days though."

"Thanks Lise."

"So, what kind of mess have you got yourself into now, Harrison?" Joe asked, with a sort of relieved, yet not surprised look on his face.

"Well, you know me, guys. It just wouldn't be trouble if I wasn't at the centre of it, would it?"

"No, I guess not," Lisa said. "We're just glad you're alright."

"I'll be out of here soon anyway."

"That's cool," Joe replied. "We were pretty shook up when we heard the news."

Joe looked anxious, as if he were screaming inside; something was eating away at him. Maybe he heard something about what happened back at the flat, but he held back as Lisa was still with us, so that was off the cards.

That was one of the many things I loved about those two – their very caring nature. So many people just go through life coasting along, not giving a thought to anyone else, but these two really were different.

"Any word form Lilly, Harrison?" Joe asked.

"I'm not sure she even knows I'm here."

"She might be worried, Harrison," he suggested.

"Chance would be a fine thing," I replied. "I've not heard that much in the last few days either."

"Harrison, you should at least let her know," Lisa said. "If she still loves you, she might even come to visit you."

"And finish the job, you mean?"

"Just text her."

"Ok Lise, you twisted my arm."

After they'd left, I decided to bite the bullet, so to speak, and send Lilly a message.

She'd heard about it from her brother, but she wasn't going to come and see me as that would probably end up starting another fire.

Probably wise, even if it was a little heartless of her.

I do wonder though, how Craig had come to hear about this, and I can't say that I'm not suspicious, but I was never one for conjecture.

Alarm bells were ringing.

And there's no such thing as coincidence.

I'd finally made it back to the flat and, surprisingly, Lilly wasn't there either. At least it meant that I might get a little respite before I went back to work.

I gave Mike an update on the situation too, and he said I could take the rest of the week, and come back on the following Monday, if I felt up to it. That'll give me a chance to catch up on shit telly (telly in general, that is) and maybe eat some half decent food before I got back on the grind. I hoped the kids had been keeping up with their work while I'd been gone. I really didn't have time to be going over old material when I got back.

Peace wasn't on the agenda though. I heard a knock at my door and anxiously made my way over to open it.

It was Craig.

Had he come to finish what he'd started? He was on his own though, so perhaps he just wanted to "talk".

Let's see what he has to say.

"Hey Craig, what's up?"

"Can I come in?"

"Sure."

"I heard about what happened. I'm sorry, man, but glad you're alright. I know that you and I were never going to braid each other's hair, but I wouldn't wish that on anyone."

Not having spent a lot of time with Craig, it was difficult to get a read on him. As much as I would have loved to have said something, I needed to be certain that I had the right person.

"Well yeah, that's true, so what can I do for you, Craig?"

"I just came to grab a few of Lilly's clothes. She's going to be staying at mine for a few days. I think she will stop by soon though, she still seems to be worried about you, for some reason."

"Bedroom's that way," I said.

"Right, I'm heading out."

"Ok, lovely to see you."

"Take care of yourself, Harrison."

Part of me couldn't help but think there might have been a hidden message in there somewhere, almost as if I hadn't seen the last of my recent troubles. I had a very odd feeling that I was going to find out either way.

Monday came back around, and I was back at work. Mike kept his word too and slowly eased me back into the swing of things with a nice light workload. It was good to have something else to focus on, something other than all the outside drama that followed me everywhere.

A few more days passed and I had a text from Joe – just checking in, I guess, and he wanted to stop by.

"Hey Joe, how you doing?"

"Meh, I needed to fucking escape for a few hours, man. How are you holding up?"

"Oh dear, that doesn't sound good," I said. "I'm cool though, recovering nicely, I think. You know you're my second visitor since I left the hospital?"

"Oh, really, that's cool, who else dropped by?"

"Craig, funnily enough."

"Oh shit, really?"

"Yeah Joe, less intense than outside the bar, that's for sure; he didn't really speak, he just came over to pick up some of Lilly's things. I guess she's going to be staying away for a few more days." I said, kind of relaxed at the thought. I really didn't have the strength to deal with this right now.

"I'm sure we'll have to air one or two things out eventually as I'm not sure the dust has settled yet, and most likely there will be a lot more to come."

"He was only here for about ten minutes," I added, "and then he left. Looked me dead in the eyes and spouted some bullshit about not wishing what happened to me on anyone. Somehow, I wasn't really sold."

"Well Harrison, I couldn't imagine why the hell you would be." Joe seemed bemused at the thought.

"What about you?" I asked. "You looked like you wanted to scream out loud when you came to visit me in hospital the other day."

"Ah, I was just thinking about the other night, in the flat. I wanted to ask you if you had heard much, but I didn't wanna worry Lisa."

"I understand," I said. "She has enough on her mind, I'm sure. But I've not heard anything yet, although I'm pretty sure that the two events are linked somehow. Coincidences just don't happen. That's bullshit."

"Yeah, I get that, Harrison. I'm sure things will come to light soon enough."

"You're damn right," I said. "But what's up with you?" I asked. "Why so meh today?"

"Lisa is super hormonal right now and I just needed to escape her for a bit, you know? She's driving me a little crazy, and I'm suffering a little from cabin fever and had to get out of the flat. So how the hell is the new office anyway, Harrison?"

"Yeah, it's good, Joe. Great to have something to take my mind off things, and Mike made good on his word and has kept my workload light too."

"Sounds cool," Joe said. "Looking forward to a break, not that we'll be resting."

"Ha, yeah, you can forget about that one for a few years – say eighteen, maybe?" I replied. "Aside from the whole expectancy sensation, it must be moving day soon, right? And how is that all shaping up now? Is Lise all good with it now?"

"Yeah, we're moving in next week, actually," Joe replied. "Pretty much all packed too – just gotta find a decent moving company. I can't be bothered with that crap, and there's no way I'm letting Lisa lift even a tea bag."

"That's cool of you," I said. "Lisa will be happy; she can relax if someone else can handle the bulk of the work for you both."

"I suppose you may be right there," Joe replied. "Although I'm not sure that would stop her. You've met her, right?"

"You guys are gonna be great, man."

"Thanks Harrison," Joe said. "We'll have you guys over once we're settled."

"Cool, I can't wait to see the place."

"Ok, I should probably make a move, buddy. I'm sure the girl needs to be fed soon – I might need to grab something on the way back for her. She can be a bit of a diva otherwise."

"Yeah, I don't doubt it," I said. "Ok man, see you soon. Tell Lisa I said hi."

"Will do, see you soon, bro."

GREY SKIES, WITH A CHANCE OF DOMESTIC

Back at work, things were still going pretty great; the students were doing well and I finally felt like I was beginning to get back on top again. Mike was still happy too, which I thought was a pretty good fuckin' result after the last few weeks. He'd been great, although I wasn't going to mention that as it would only go to his head, and I couldn't have that. Not at all.

Still no word from the girl. I guess maybe this could be the end of the road...

Maybe she'd come over when she was ready, but for the time being, I would respect her space and give her some time to herself. It's not as if I've not made the effort to reach out to her – countless calls and texts, that's got to count for something. I don't expect any sympathy at all, but if I can try to salvage what's left of the relationship, I will... despite all of our bullshit.

What is a boy to do? To quote The Clash, "Should I stay, or should I go?" I had no idea how this would end up playing out, but I was sure that I'd find out soon enough.

I came straight home after work and I saw a light on inside. *This should be interesting.* Anxiously, I made my way inside.

It was Lilly.

"Hi, Harrison."

She looked sad and pissed off, both at the same time. Her eyes looked as if she had literally given up; I could probably understand after all our ups and downs. She was never shy about her emotions; not the passive-aggressive type. If there's something on her mind, I'd definitely hear about it. And that was one of her greatest qualities, never shying away from her words.

"Hey, Lilly."

"Hey, Harrison, how are you feeling?" she replied. "I'm sorry that I didn't come by sooner, but I've been a little frustrated and annoyed with you still."

A little self-absorbed, maybe. I wonder if she still gives a shit about me. Does she still give a shit about us?

"Yeah, I'd actually picked up on that through my attempts at reaching out to you. Be that as it may, a visit would have been nice. I was shot you know. Twice."

"What the fuck do you want from me, Harrison?" she snapped. "I don't owe you anything!"

"No, Lilly, I suppose you don't. You made that very clear when you came to visit me whilst I was in the hospital. Oh wait, you didn't visit me at all. Did you?"

"Fuck you!" she screamed. "Do you even remember why I'm so fucking pissed at you?"

Ah, there she is. That's the Lilly I remember. Not as cute and cuddly as she looks from the outside.

"Yeah, Lilly I do – just about."

Shit. This is the first time I've given it any real thought since it happened. I can see why she's so mad now.

"Did you sleep with her?"

"Did I sleep with who?"

"Don't play dumb with me. You know who the fuck I'm talking about! Mary."

"I don't even know how it happened, Lilly."

"How what happened, Harrison? Did anything happen between you two?"

"What? No Lilly."

"So why would you be calling out her name whilst we're in bed the other night?"

"I don't know, Lilly. I really don't. Nothing is going on with her though. I haven't seen or heard from Mary in years, since we broke up."

I wasn't sure if I should mention Mary's little visit the other night.

At this point, I didn't know if I may somehow end up making things worse for myself by giving her too little. Lilly would always draw her own conclusions, with or without my input, and that's the way she's always been.

Strong-willed and stubborn as hell. Good qualities to a point, I guess, but you must hear both sides of the story.

I suppose that depends on both of us, and how well we can recover from the drama. If we can recover at all. An hour or so had passed and we were still going at it.

"So, what's your excuse then, Harrison? Please tell me because I'm just dying to hear it. I really am."

"I really don't have one, Lilly," I replied, "other than she was a part of my life a long time ago and she's still in my subconscious, I guess. That doesn't mean that I have any feelings for her."

"I don't know, Harrison. Do you?"

"Are you kidding me, Lilly?" I said. "You should know me pretty well by this point; we've been together long enough and I'm always with you, or with Joe, and great as he is, I'm not going to run off with him. I'm not a fan of beards for starters."

"So, you still like pussy then? I suppose that's a good start."

I wondered if her making a joke meant she might be calming down a bit now.

"Of course I do, especially yours."

"Well, I'm not sure you'll be dining at the Y again for a while, if at all."

"Lilly, how do I know you haven't been messing around while I've been lying in hospital?"

"Why would I be the one screwing around?"

"Well, you didn't bother to come and see me while I was in the hospital," I said, "so I have to ask whether you even give a shit about us…"

"I'm here, aren't I?"

She really makes me laugh; she's here in body but her heart isn't.

"You're 'here', Lilly?"

"Yeah, Harrison."

"What the hell is that supposed to mean, Lilly? You're only here so you can pack a damn bag for wherever it is you're going." I could feel myself getting more frustrated by this little visit.

"Yeah, I suppose you're right," she replied, "and now I'm heading out again. And don't bother trying to get in touch with me either."

"Well, where are you going, Lilly?"

"Somewhere you're not," she snarled. "Right now, no I really couldn't care about us. Harrison, after all of our bullshit, I think we could use a bit of a break from each other, and the relationship. Lately, I think we'd just be doing more harm than good, and that's not fun for either of us."

In my head, I was weighing up my options, good and bad, and thought that maybe this could be the best thing for us. I didn't want to keep going around in circles with her every other week. This was far too much strain on the two of us.

Honestly, I'm exhausted.

"So, what have you been doing for the last few days then, while you were busy not seeing me?" I asked. "Just scheming to pack up and leave without telling me? Would you even have said anything had I not come back?"

"Probably not, no."

Pretty cold. I don't think that anyone deserves that.

"Damn, Lilly, I might have to open the freezer door a little. I need to warm the place up a bit after that."

"Well, I love that you still have your sense of humour. Maybe you can laugh yourself to sleep while you're sat here in the flat all alone. I love that you've left my message on the wall too. You know it suits you."

She really has had enough, I reckon, and I was wondering if I could really blame her, despite the fact that nothing had happened. Why the hell was she in my head anyway? And I should come clean and tell her about the other night too, even though it's going to hurt her more. I have to be honest with her.

"Try and see this from my perspective, Harrison," she said. "Can we really carry on like this?"

"Sure, why not? We've survived for a few years like this, haven't we?"

"Barely, Harrison."

That comment really made me stop and think; surviving was all it had been. Who was I trying to fool?

"We have, Harrison, you're right," she said, "but is that really enough? I need so much more than that, I need to know that you can give me everything I need to make me feel whole."

"You might be right, Lilly. I don't know, though. We have always had our ups and downs, and it's normal for couples to overcome that day-to-day bullshit."

"I love how you're trying to downplay it. How many 'ups and downs' have we had? I'm not sure that I would refer to us as a normal couple, Harrison. We're pretty dysfunctional as relationships go."

"Most of them are, Lilly, aren't they?" I said. "You never know what goes on behind closed doors. The perfect couple could be just as screwed up as the next. You just don't know."

"You're probably right," she replied, "but I don't care about them. We're talking about us, and I'm not sure how this is going to last, Harrison. I really don't know how it can work anymore."

"Lilly, there's something I have to tell you about the other night."

"What now?"

Her expression seemed to sink even lower. I had that awful feeling in my chest that this was going to be the end for us.

"There is something that I've not told you about Mary, about the other night."

I could see her playing around with an old photo of us. I couldn't tell if she was going to pack it in her bag or toss it out the window.

"Are you fucking kidding me right now, Harrison?" she snapped again. "What is it? Just tell me. I don't know how much more of this I can take."

"She came to see me the other night."

"WHAT?"

"Are you kidding me right now, Harrison?"

The photo that Lilly was playing with was now flying straight for my head."Nothing happened, Lilly."

She stared at me in disbelief.

"What the fuck did she want then, if it wasn't your dick inside her once more?"

"She tried to force herself in the flat and tried to kiss me," I replied, "but I pushed her away and sent her packing. She was here less than two minutes."

"I'm not even mad, Harrison. I know what she's like, but thank you for telling me. It means something that you didn't keep that one to yourself. Anything else happen while I was gone then, Harrison?"

She made her way for the door, crying and cursing my name some more as she left. I tried to run after her, but she screamed at me and told me not to bother. Something told me she knew a lot more than she was letting on, and I needed answers.

As she ran out the door, I wondered if I would ever see her again.

SO, WHAT HAPPENS NOW?

dropped Joe a quick text to see if I could sway him with the prospect of a few weeknight cold ones.

Success, we are GO for beers!

As I anxiously made my way down to the river, I wondered what other excitement the night might bring. Never a dull moment.

"There he is. How are you doing, buddy?" he asked, apprehensively. "Have you managed to get yourself into trouble again?"

He's got his wits about him tonight this one, hasn't he?

"Joe, I have no idea what you're talking about. I am an angel – a model citizen, in fact."

We both knew that was bullshit, so I try a different approach.

"Well, it's funny that you should ask because that one has a very interesting story behind it that involves smashed glass and a very angry girlfriend."

We made our way over to the bar and ordered a couple of beers.

"So she actually made the effort to come and see you then?" he said. "That's gotta be a positive thing, right?"

"Well, not exactly, Joe. She only really came over to pack a bag, and then she left. Well, after a brief and heated debate over us, and where we were going."

"Damn, man," Joe said. "I can't imagine that would have gone as planned, and I can tell by the look on your face that it didn't. How's my aim?"

"Pretty good, Joe," I replied. "Why do you think we're out tonight? Thanks for coming out too. I didn't wanna drag you out as I know that you have your hands full with Lisa and everything."

"That's cool. You know I'll be there if you want to talk, or grab a beer. I'm here if you need anything, you know that."

"Thanks Joe, I appreciate that."

"So, how are you and Lisa doing these days? Is everything ok with the bump too?"

"Yeah, she's great, man. Thanks for asking. We're doing good. We're moving into the flat next week too."

"That's great, Joe," I said. "I'm really happy for the both of you. Let me know if you need help with the crib, won't you? I am an engineer after all."

"You are, aren't you?" Joe replied. "That may come in handy in the future. I'll need someone to come and fix my fridge after Lisa keeps raiding it with her midnight cravings."

"Anything you need though, man. Seriously."

"Cheers Harrison," Joe said, then he paused, unsure. "So, how did the little visit from Lilly really go? Dramatic?"

"You know, it wasn't actually, Joe, and that's a little surprising really, considering how we were going at it. Then again, our neighbours are most likely used to it by this stage. It's almost like a bi-weekly ritual now, you know? Some people go to church and have a nice Sunday roast, Lilly and I scream at each other and smash things across the room."

Mostly just photographs, and the occasional plate for good measure.

"But something's gotta give, you know," Joe said. "How long are you two going to run around in circles, dancing around the same bullshit?"

I sat and meditated on that for a moment and thought about how much sense he was making at that very moment; how long could we go on masquerading as a "happy" couple, trying to tear each other's eyes out every other week while the neighbours probably sat there with the police on speed dial for fear that one of us might kill the other?

He made a good point. Both of us seriously needed to re-evaluate what the hell we were doing together, because we were just destroying each other.

I felt that, day by day, a little piece of me was disappearing. From the look in Lilly's eyes whenever I saw her, I had a feeling that Lilly felt the same too, and you'd think that the notion of that alone would be a no brainer for a quick escape.

"You're right. We do need to sit and talk properly and figure out what we're doing and where we're going, if anywhere, because right now the only thing I can see is a pathway to destruction."

"Sometimes, Joe, I think that you're a much better voice of reason than I could ever be, and you always seem to do the right thing."

"Thanks Harrison, but unfortunately, that's not always the case. It's always nice to get some different perspective when you've got so much on your mind. It's so much easier to look at the situation from the outside. Too often, your judgement is clouded when your head's moving a million miles a minute."

"After everything I've heard," Joe said, "maybe a clean break is the best thing for you guys. Or maybe what you really need is something like a zero-hours contract girlfriend, you know? Just something nice and casual to help you with your transition back into the wild."

Not the worst idea he's had.

"Right now, I'd really enjoy some 'me time'; just peace and a drama-free existence. Whatever happens between the two of us, we still have to make arrangements for the flat too, as we're still under contract right now."

"Well, whatever happens, I'm sure that you will survive this. You've been through the wringer the last few months, but you will get through this. You always do."

He was right too.

I've had one hell of a rollercoaster ride these last few weeks and things are finally beginning to look a lot better. Admittedly, there are still some loose ends that would need to be tied up, but things aren't as bad as before.

Whichever route I decided to take, though, it was important that I didn't let my heart outweigh my ability to deal with reason. Yes, I love her, but was that really going to be enough for me?

Was it enough for her?

There are plenty of people that love one another but can't be together, and that's why they drift apart.

"I know what you mean," Joe said. "Just try not to stress it too much, you know? That's easier said than done, but just see how things go after a few days. Just give her some time."

That wasn't a bad idea, to credit Joe. I did think it was best to let things lie, and not make any decisions when mad.

"Good plan," I said. "You're making a lot of sense today – what's going on? Are you on some new medication?"

"I know. Weird, right? Especially considering I've been woken up early to the dulcet sounds of Lisa and her morning sickness the last couple of weeks."

"Ah Joe," I smiled, "you have so much to look forward to."

"I know. I'm looking forward to those fun-filled nights. So long sleep – it was just swell knowing you were always there when I needed you the most." Joe sighed a little as he meditated on what the future held in store.

"You two are going to be just fine, man. You're great together, and you're gonna be incredible parents too."

"Thanks man. It will be scary as hell, but I'm sure we'll figure it all out." There he was thinking again; a dangerous moment. "So, Harrison, I gotta ask you… what did you do to piss her off so much?"

"Um, well, I might have called out someone else's name while we were in bed the last time she was here… after my night out in the Final Final the other week."

"Shit man, that's um, yeah. Fuck. Who was it you called out?"

"Whose name?"

"Yeah."

"Mary," I replied, "which is weird considering that I hadn't heard from the woman in forever. But I guess that she's still floating about in my psyche somewhere."

"Damn, man. I'll say."

"What's stranger than that, though, is that she paid me a little visit a few days before I was shot. Part of me was thinking I really wished I would have had my way with her that night, even though I knew things were already somewhat contentious in my personal life. A lesser man would have cracked, and I'm a little surprised that I didn't."

"Shit, really!?" Joe exclaimed, seemingly more shocked than I was.

"Yeah Joe, nothing happened, though. Well, that's not strictly true. She did try to pounce as I opened the door and have her way with me, but I didn't let it happen. Admittedly, it was a struggle."

"I bet, man," Joe said. "I remember Mary. She was smoking hot."

"Yeah, she's still hot as hell, but it's just the rest of it that was an issue for us, Joe. Our heads were never in it, even if our genitals were."

"Harrison, you two should have just stayed as the whole zero-hours thing. You were so much better off that way, I think."

"Zero-hours contract girlfriend," I said. "I'm going to steal that, Joe."

"You're welcome. Just don't tell Lisa that's my line, otherwise she'll probably go all Lorena Bobbitt on me while I'm asleep. Did you tell her about Mary stopping by?" Joe asked.

"Yeah, I told her," I replied, anxiously wiping my brow while reliving that moment. "She wasn't best pleased, given current events and what had tipped her over the edge already, but she appreciated the fact that I had told her and was straight up about it."

"That's good that you were upfront, Harrison. You don't wanna be holding anything back, especially at this stage. Was she really ok about it, though?"

"Well, not massively," I replied, clutching my head in my hands, "which is understandable, but truth be told, I think she'd just run out of energy. That was pretty much when she left, but I'm sure I haven't heard the last of it. I've always gone with my gut feeling and it's never been wrong. Knowing Lilly the way I do, there will likely be some kind of dramatic encore, you know?"

"I got to go in a minute," Joe said, "but I wanted to ask you: did you ever hear anything else about who might have dropped by for a little Q&A in the kitchen that time? Or, better still, who shot you after leaving the bar?"

"No, man, that one still has a big question mark over it. I'll gct to the bottom of it though, one way or another."

"I hope so, Harrison. That will be a massive weight off your mind, I'm sure. With or without Lilly, whatever other shit goes down, you need closure on that one."

"Absolutely, Joe, and I won't stop until I do."

I'M NOT SURE THE DUST HAS SETTLED, YET

Things were really looking up in the office, and I had to say, I was really enjoying it. I had all the work that I could handle, and Mike was really impressed with how I'd taken to it after the last few weeks. But it wasn't all work and no fun, after all I needed to treat myself sometimes. So I decided to take myself out to dinner and have a few drinks at the Loch.

I thought I would make a conscious effort to keep a low profile and stay out of trouble for a change.

After I'd eaten, I'd spotted a familiar face coming my way.

There she was again.

It was Charlotte. She was wearing this cute little tank top that hugged her bust nicely, knee-high boots, a short skirt, and fishnet stockings. *A look that could cure cancer.*

A part of me thought I should just finish my beer and leave, but something told me to stick around. I was looking about the room, just people-watching, and she spotted me. Busted.

I had been doing so well too.

"Hey trouble, what brings you here?"

"Well, Charlotte, if it isn't my favourite hangover cure, the bringer of coffee and food. How are you?"

"I'm great, thanks."

"Cool. How is the writing coming along? All good, I hope."

"Wow," she said. "I'm surprised you remembered!"

"Why wouldn't I remember? I'd like to think I'm pretty attentive."

"Very modest too." She smiled, cheekily.

"Of course, Charlotte, always."

"It's going really well though. Thank you for asking. I'm about a third of the way through my first draft, right now."

"That's amazing, Charlotte. Just make sure you keep at it, won't you?"

"Of course," she said, "I don't wanna be dealing with the sleazy hungover type for the rest of my life, y'know? Present company excluded, of course."

"Aw, thanks Charlotte, but how do you know I don't fall into that category?"

"I don't know. I think there's something about you. I guess it's your eyes – they look very kind."

"Thank you," I replied with a cheeky smile across my face. "People tell me that my eyes are my best feature, but I don't see it."

"That's cute, I like that. I might use that in my writing, if that's ok with you?"

Damn, is she flirting with me right now? I feel a little conflicted; I'm not sure if I need another decision to make that's going to require any more of my tiny brain's resource. The little mouse powering my brain is getting more tired as of late.

"Sure thing," I said. "You can use it so long as I get credit in the writing, or at the very least a drink at some point."

What am I doing? Did I just ask this girl out?

"So, how has Harrison been lately? I haven't seen you in a while, now."

"Now that's a hostile question, Charlotte. I've had a rough couple of weeks: I've been shot, tied up and I think my girlfriend and I are finished."

"Oh Harrison, poor baby. That sounds awful! Aside from being tied up. You can tie me up, you know, if you want to."

Damn, now that is a nice thought.

I'm not sure I'm going to be getting a lot of sleep tonight with that image floating around in my head. The way she was looking at me, she was totally going in for the kill right now, and I wasn't sure whether I should stop her or not, given that I could use some friendly company.

She had kissed me, and I did feel guilty, but I would be lying if I'd said I didn't enjoy it… a little.

Now, all I have is this image of her being tied up, all defenceless, while I have my way and just take her.

"You know, Harrison, you do have nice eyes, and you're a great kisser too."

"You're not so bad yourself, Charlotte, for a budding writer."

"Of course, you can grab a drink too. How about tonight, trouble, back at my place? I'm only around the corner."

"Charlotte, there's nothing I would love more than to join you for a few more back at yours, but my head is all messed up right now and it just wouldn't be fair on you."

"Don't worry about fair, I'm not looking for anything long-term. I have enough to keep me busy, writing-wise and work too. I would rather you stopped by and had your way with me 'til I couldn't walk, plus it would give my wrist a break too, you know?"

I think I may have to take this lady up on her offer; I could always use another drink, and a little exercise wouldn't do me any harm either.

"Charlotte, you have a very naughty mouth, don't you?"

"Don't forget, talented."

"Talented, how so?"

"I'm pretty sure I already knew how that would go down," but it's always nice to have clarification on these things.

"Well, why don't you come back with me, and maybe I can show you?"

She makes a pretty good pitch, I have to say.

The only thing that people hate more than being lied to is the truth, and I can't lie to myself.

Things are pretty crappy right now and I'm not sure they will get better. Sometimes it's just nice having someone there, even if it's just to listen and make you feel special, and wanted.

A few more drinks later and I felt as if we were beginning to really connect. Aesthetics aside, she seemed to be so down to earth and open, like no other person I've ever come across. All the while, in my head I'm thinking about the Lilly situation, but realistically I think we already knew where we were headed.

A long time coming, you might say.

As much as I love Lilly – and even after everything, I'm still absolutely nuts about her, which is probably the saddest thing about it – we still went at it and tore each other's eyes out, screaming the place down until three in the morning. It shouldn't have to be work, but with all the other stuff that's happened with Craig, and the other drama that seems to follow me everywhere I go, I'm starting to believe that being on my own might be the best thing for me.

"Charlotte, are you trying to get me drunk and take advantage of me? Because if you are, I'm going to head to the bar."

"Well, Mr," she smiled, "what if I am?"

I feel my resolve weakening right now.

"You look as though you could use a release, Harrison."

"Well, Charlotte, I may end up just letting you, and I'm not too sure if that's a good thing or not right now. I might end up crying in your arms until 4am, thinking about what a mess I've gotten myself into."

Judging by the way that she was glaring at me, she didn't care about any of that.

She was hungry. There was no possible way to hide it. She was beautiful, and she could see that I felt that.

My eyes really gave the game away more than words could.

"Shall we make tracks then, handsome?"

"Please be gentle," I said. "I've been hurt before."

"Don't worry, baby. Charlotte will take care of you."

I'm not sure I remember being chased so much. I would be lying if I said that I wasn't enjoying it. It's always nice to be wanted, even if it's only something that will end up as a night of fun.

"Charlotte, what have you done to me? I'm starting to get a little hard right now."

"Really, can I see?"

Before I knew it, she was gently tugging away at me while we waited for the taxi.

We made our way inside, she opened the door and dragged me to the bedroom and pushed me onto the bed.

I grabbed that ass and pulled her upright, taking that top off and slowly sliding off those boots of hers, and everything else but her stockings.

Before I knew it, I was inside of her. An hour or so had passed, and she was still riding me, like one of those mechanical bulls in a bar, and before long she'd passed out in my arms.

"Damn, Charlotte, that was hot. I think I may have to take you out to lunch sometime soon. I have to make a move though. Unfortunately, I have a lot on today."

"Sure thing, Harrison."

I wasn't just saying that either. I really did enjoy myself, and she knew it too, and I wasn't afraid to show it.

"I'll see you soon, big boy." As I was leaving, we kissed, and she handed me a folded cocktail napkin. Inside, her number was written in red lipstick.

Cute.

Just as I was making my way back to grab my train, I got a text from Lilly.

"*Where the fuck are you? We need to talk NOW!*"

Just another day in paradise.

THE TRUTH SHALL SET YOU FREE

I had a good feeling about today; the sun was shining and I had a nice spring in my step. Charlotte was right, I did need a release, and I felt as if I could think more clearly now, so much clearer than I have in a long time.

Joe had just texted me too. Mum had just been for a check-up, and they had news and wanted to share something with me.

"Hey Joe, how are you doing?"

"Great, man," he said. "We just came back from the hospital this morning. Lisa had her first scan and the baby is all healthy and she's doing great too."

"Coffee?"

"Sure, thanks Joe."

"Here, you wanna see?" he asked. "It's not HD, but you can make out the head and bum at least."

"Sure man."

"Where's Mum, she alright?"

"Yeah, she's great," he said, "just having a little snooze right now."

"So, is it a boy or a girl?"

"We're gonna have a little boy, Harrison."

He looked so happy as he was showing me the scan. I can't remember the last time I saw him that pleased with anything – the way his eyes lit up was so nice to see.

At that moment, I really envied him too. I'd always wanted that for myself; a beautiful little family of my own. Maybe someday, I will. We never know what the future will hold – I might end up shacked up with Charlotte for the next few months.

"Ah, Joe, I'm so happy for you both," I smiled and was looking forward to hearing more. "I bet you can't wait to meet the little guy now, Joe? You must be real excited."

"Yeah, Harrison. We're both crazy anxious right now. Lisa's got me reading about ten thousand baby books. Amongst all my other work stuff that I'm doing, I'm pretty fried. I'll be happy if he's a week overdue at the end of all this; it'll give me more time to catch up on the endless mountain of paperwork I have."

"Understandable," I said, "there's never enough time in the day, Joe. And there never will be. Especially with the little guy. But you two will figure it out. You'll have the parent thing down. I know it."

"Thanks Harrison."

"One thing I gotta ask, Joe. Bit of a weird one, I know…"

"Go for it, man. Anything you need, you know that."

"Would you mind being my emergency contact?" I asked. "I feel after everything, especially the most recent events, that I should probably have one, and I feel that you're the only one I can really count on."

"Sure thing, Harrison. I can't say I blame you, man. Put both of us down."

"Thanks Joe. That means a lot, knowing that I can count on you. Have you guys had any thoughts on names yet? You're gonna call him Logan, right?"

"Hmm, not yet, buddy. I'll probably end up just going with whatever Lisa wants to be fair."

"You're gonna call him Logan though, right?"

"Ha, we'll see, Harrison."

"I gotta run," I said. "Great to see you though. I'm so happy for you guys. Tell Lisa I said hi and I'll be over again to check on you guys soon."

"Cool, take it easy," Joe said. "I wanna hear more about the Lilly thing too. When you have some more time, we need a proper catch up."

"Oh, you will, my old friend. We've much to talk about, Joseph. Just watch this space."

"I look forward to it, Professor."

I suppose I should probably catch up with Lilly and see what she has to say this time. I can't think what she could be so mad about now.

I arrived back at the flat, anxiously awaiting a girl that used to be my girlfriend, expecting to see her sitting there, waiting to tear me a new one.

"I came by to see you last night Harrison, where the fuck where you?"

She's already in a mood, fantastic.

"Good morning, Lilly," I said. "Nice to see you. So, are you going to tell me what you want? Or shall we just stand in the hallway and scream at each other? I do have a lot of stuff I'd like to do today."

"I know that we didn't really have a chance to sit down and talk properly the last time I was here, and I just wanted to speak to you without screaming."

"You mean talking at me without me being given half a chance to get a word in?"

"Yeah, well, I'd like to say I'm sorry, Harrison, but I think we've come to the end here, don't you? I just don't think that we can keep doing this anymore, and I think I need to walk away from you, and from this."

"I'm not sure I can take any more shitty nights on the sofa either, y'know?"

"Well Harrison, you deserved it," she said. "Most of the time."

"Yeah, thanks. I'm sure I did," I replied with a sombre look about me. "Lilly, I've a question. Did you know that someone came into the flat a while ago and attacked me? You wouldn't happen to know anything about that, would you?"

"What makes you think I'd know anything about that, Harrison? What kind of person do you think I am? What did they look like?"

I could always get a pretty good read on Lilly, and something wasn't right about her expression. It almost looked as if she felt guilty, but also somewhat satisfied at the same time.

"I don't know, Lilly," I replied. "He had a ski mask on. Any ideas? It all seems a bit odd to me; you vanish for a few days and I get knocked unconscious, tied up and held at knifepoint in my own flat. Then, not long after that, I was shot. Twice. Not even a peep from you, and I haven't heard a lot from the police either, so you'll forgive me if I'm a little suspicious."

"Well, I don't know anything about that, Harrison," she said. "Even after everything, I hope you know I wouldn't do that to you…"

"I don't know anymore, Lilly," I said. "My head has been pretty screwed up over the last few weeks after everything that's gone down. Wait…

what makes you think there was more than one of them? I didn't say how many there were."

"I don't know," she replied. "I heard something, I think."

"You 'heard' something? What the fuck does that mean, Lilly?"

I could feel myself getting wound up again. Heard something from whom? Craig? His friends? Who?

She looked as if she was going to break down and maybe give me something real, hopefully something I could use to give myself some closure. Or maybe even the police so that I could move on with my life and not have to worry about any more uninvited dinner guests in my kitchen.

"I'm sorry, Harrison!" she said, finally. "I didn't know anything about it. I only asked him to scare you. I didn't want any harm to come to you. I still love you, don't you know that?"

"Are you fucking kidding me, Lilly?"

She broke down and held her head in her hands. She did look genuinely surprised that they'd gone to such lengths, to harm me, and the worst part was that I believed her too.

"You still love me? For fuck's sake, Lilly. That's cute, but you'll forgive me if I don't believe you right now."

"I understand." She didn't try to fight me any-more.

"You understand?" I snapped. "Really, now please explain to me how that could be possible, because I'd very much like to hear how. I really would."

"Ok, I don't. I have no idea what that must have felt like, Harrison. I never wanted them to do any of that stuff."

"You're right, you have absolutely no clue – to have someone break into the place and hold you at knifepoint in my own damn flat, only to get shot too, all in the space of about three weeks."

A small part of me was surprised at how remorseful she seemed, but I felt we were way too far gone to try and salvage anything. I honestly couldn't even see straight. I just don't know what she could realistically expect from me at this point.

"Damn, Lilly," I said. "I don't know what the hell to even say to you right now."

"Just say whatever you feel, Harrison. Tell me whatever's on your mind."

"I don't even know anymore, Lilly. I can't even think straight right now."

I wasn't even kidding her. I felt physically sick and, at the same time, like I wanted to scream at her and tear this fucking flat apart, but then again what good would that do me? Plus, I'd only end up having to bloody clean it up.

"I'd like you to leave, Lilly. I don't feel comfortable right now and would really appreciate some time on my own, so I can make some attempt to try and clear my head."

"Ok, Harrison, I will leave you to it, but I'm going to speak to Craig and find out everything I can from him to see what he knows, alright?" She didn't seem too convincing, but I'd hoped that she may help me to find that closure I had needed to move forward.

"Thanks, I've no doubt in my mind he knows something."

I'd told Joe the news and, not surprisingly I suppose, we'd pretty much drawn the same conclusion as to who was behind everything that had happened.

Back to work then, I guess.

A few days went by and, now that I'd had some sort of closure, I was feeling a lot better about things. Work was going great too; at least I thought it was going great. That was until Mike came looking for me, telling me there was someone waiting for me in the main reception.

This should be interesting. I wondered what could possibly sabotage my day this time. I was starting to convince myself the universe was out to get me.

It was Lilly.

"Hey, Harrison," she said. "How are you doing?"

What the hell was she doing here?

I really didn't know how much more drama I could endure, and I was pretty sure I'd had enough in the space of a few weeks to last me a lifetime. It was only recently that things were really starting to pick up again.

"I'm good," I replied. "What can I do for you, Lilly?"

"Nothing, Harrison. I just came to tell you that I'd spoken to Craig, and he came clean about everything. He was behind all of it."

Of course. Who else could it have been?

I fucking knew it. It had his name written all over it.

As much as I wanted to make a scene, I wasn't about to make trouble for myself at my place of work, even though it pained me to bite my tongue. Especially after all the good work I had been putting in, it would be a crying shame to screw it all up now.

"Thank you for telling me, Lilly," I said. "I really do appreciate that. I needed to clarify what I had already suspected anyway, and that makes a lot of sense."

"I'm sorry, Harrison… for everything."

"Me too, Lilly."

"So, what are you going to do about Craig?"

"You mean, am I going to talk to the police and help fill in the blanks after they found absolutely nothing, in terms of leads and evidence?"

"Yes, Harrison. Or are you going to settle things the old-fashioned way?"

Is she kidding me right now? Is she really trying to fish for answers and try to save his sorry ass, in some lame attempt to maybe try and justify what happened?

Unbelievable.

"I don't really know right now, Lilly. I have enough going on right now, without having to worry about dealing with your brother too."

"Ok," she said, "well, I suppose it's his mess whatever happens."

"Yes, Lilly, it is, and why should you care anyway? He's done this to himself."

"I don't know," she replied, "and I know that this is in part my fault too, so I don't have any right to try and influence your decision."

"No, you're right, you really don't, Lilly. You lost all of that when you suggested he 'scare me.'"

I could hear Mike coming down the hall and was thinking that I should probably try and wrap this up quickly. I didn't particularly want my life on display in the middle of the damn office.

"Goodbye, Harrison, good luck with the new job too. I'm sorry."

"Goodbye, Lilly, I really hope that you can find whatever it is you're looking for."

She began to well up as she hugged me and handed me her key to the flat and walked away down the hall. Given everything that had gone down over the last few weeks, I needed to consider changing flat, or at the very least getting some stronger locks. Maybe I'm just being paranoid, but it couldn't hurt.

"Man, she did not look happy, Harrison."

"Hey Mike, no she's not feeling too peachy right now."

"I can tell. Everything ok?"

"Not really," I replied. "We've just broken up."

"Shit, sorry Harrison."

"Don't worry, Mike. It's ok. It's been brewing for a while."

"Well, if you need to get out of here early, let me know, right? We'll hit a bar!"

"Thanks Mike, you're a star."

"Anytime."

It was getting near the end of the day and I had decided to take Mike up on his offer, probably a good thing as I could see him making his way over.

"Harrison, stop what you're doing. Let's get the fuck out of here; beer waits for no man!"

"Alright Mike, you twisted my arm. Let's go – adventure beckons."

I could get used to leaving around two every day.

We'd hit a few bars by the university before we ended up in the Final Final. After sinking a few together and having a good catch-up, Mike left at around six and I made my way on to another bar. Even though it was a school night, I felt that I owed it to myself to let my hair down properly and have a chance to regroup and collect myself.

Eventually, I'd found myself in my favourite spot: the Loch. That place always had my heart. There was something quite relaxing about it that made it hard to stay away from.

I had grabbed myself another cold one and posted myself up by the window where I could watch the world go by. I always enjoyed just taking a minute to people-watch; I'd always found it quite cathartic.

Just as I was finishing my beer, who should I spot walking through the door?

Amy.

Fuck, she looked amazing. I just hoped she wasn't working that night. It would be great to catch up with her properly over a few drinks.

When she walked into the room, I could feel myself lighting up and I thought she could feel it too. Given my terrible poker face, it was pretty obvious, but I didn't see sense in trying to hide it. If I liked her, then why wouldn't I show it? Life's too fucking boring not to try.

"Hey Amy, how are you doing? Long time, no see!"

"Hey Harrison, what's going on?"

"I've seen better days, Amy."

"Why so sad, dude?"

"Lilly and I broke up today."

"Oh man, I'm sorry to hear that," she said, "but it sounds like you were too good for her anyway, from everything I've heard about you guys."

"Thanks Amy. That's sweet of you to say."

Damn, even when she's consoling me, she even seems to somehow make sympathy sound sexy.

"So, what brings you here tonight," I asked. "Are you off?"

"The beer, Harrison. The beer! So, are you going to ask me to join you or what?"

"Sure Amy, sit that little bum down."

After a few more beers and some food, the night was shaping up to be pretty great. It was really cool just catching up on lost time with her. As I thought about how great she looked, gazing her up and down, I think she knew the signals she was giving off. Whenever she walked in the room, I felt all the hairs on the back of my neck stand up, that real butterfly sensation.

On the plus side, whatever I got up to now, there was only a minimal risk of me getting myself into trouble. Although I shouldn't be overconfident about that one; it would usually manage to find me easily enough on its own.

"Harrison, do you want me to grab my camera so you can take a few photos?"

"I'm sorry Amy," I said, "that outfit though."

It was plain to see, my eyes were pretty much popping out of my head.

"I was being serious," she said, smiling. "You can take pictures of me if you like, maybe in the bedroom though. It will be fun. We can do anything you want."

Before I could say "action", she'd leant in pulled me towards her by my collar, and kissed me.

"Harrison, I've been wanting to do that for a few years."

"You know it's been about four years since we saw each other last?"

"Shit, seriously?" I said. That was not good. We have a lot of lost time to make up for. "I enjoyed that. I could use a lot more of those too."

"Mmm definitely, you and me both, Harrison."

"Do you wanna go grab a coffee or something, Amy? I've been out since two and I need to put the beer down for a little, I think."

"We could do, sure," she replied. "But I'd rather go back to yours; my heating is broken and it's just me all alone in that big old flat by the river."

Well, that escalated quickly. I had always been crazy about that girl, I think she knew it, and I don't think I could afford to let her slip away again.

I don't want to wonder what my life might have been like if I hadn't pushed for more.

"Ok, handsome, are you ready?"

"Lead the way, Amy."

When we got back to mine, things started heating up nicely. I'd barely managed to finish my coffee before she threw me on the sofa and ripped my shirt off, and then dragged my jeans off.

She took that dress off and kicked her boots to the wall, leaving just that cute little backless dress and her underwear. She went to work on my shaft, just enough so I was primed for her.

I grabbed her from behind, kissing her neck, moving slowly down her back as I unhooked her bra, Then slowly took her shoulders out of the straps and paused as I watched it fall.

I slowly shifted, kissing her neck as I moved further down her body, with her trembling at my every touch.

Pretty soon, she was on top of me, riding me like nobody else ever has. I really felt as if our bodies were in perfect sync at that moment.

Each part of her body responded so well to my every touch, and mine did too; it was pretty electric.

It was almost as if she were made just for me.

It had been a while since I'd been in a flat that had some decent vocals running through it, screams of pleasure rather than yelling. We went at it until we were trembling and both in need of a break.

"Damn, Amy, I haven't been fucked that hard since I was an altar boy."

As we lay there, I traced my fingers upon her body, slowly moving up and down. I watched her as she wriggled, feeling a tingling sensation all over.

"Thanks Harrison. I don't think I've been fucked like that in… forever."

"Well, it's always nice to know that my work is appreciated, and I'm not immune to such kind words. Especially when they're so true. But Amy, there's something I've been meaning to ask you."

"What is it, baby?"

"Why the hell did we not do that sooner?"

"Mmm, I don't know, Harrison, but I'm not sure that we should leave it so long until the next time."

"Definitely not."

"Harrison, I have a question for you. It's very important too."

"Anything," I said, "what is it?"

"Can we go again, please?"

"What kind of a man would I be if I were to deny a beautiful lady such a request?"

"A stupid one, now shut up and fuck me."

"Mmm, I love it when you tell me what to do."

HAPPILY EVER AFTER

It was a beautiful Saturday morning; the leaves were beginning to fall, the sun was shining, and autumn was finally coming.

I was off to meet Joe for breakfast at the usual spot, then, in the evening, I thought I might cook Amy something extra special for dinner.

It seemed as if my luck might have finally changed for the better. Work was better than ever; I'd just been promoted, and I was looking at buying a bigger flat closer to the city with a view overlooking the riverside. Success really is the best revenge; if only all the nonbelievers could see me now.

There I was, laughing to myself in the middle of the streets like a fucking crazy person, but I never really took the time to stop and take stock of how great things really were, really savour the moment every chance I got.

Everything was falling into place, and I couldn't have been happier. It felt strange, knowing that, after all that had happened lately, I hadn't even thought it was possible, but it was though. I really was happy.

Joe had signed the contract and moved into the new place with Lisa, and he'd just made partner in the firm. The baby was nearly due as well, so I couldn't be more pleased for the two of them; they were nearly a family at last. If anyone deserved it, those two did.

Town was very quiet that morning, which was unusual for a Saturday; it looked beautiful, with a little ambience. It was ever so much more tranquil than the chaos you had to endure on your typical Monday commute, things were that much more chilled out.

It felt so good, knowing that Lilly and I had come to a *relatively* amicable end to our relationship, and I could start my new life with Amy without anything looming over me. Well, I say amicable… as good as it could have been, I guess.

Despite our coasting along, from time to time, it was good to feel the pain. Even if it hurt so badly you wanted to tear your fucking eyes out.

No loose ends at least.

I could really see myself spending the rest of my life with Amy; she was the only one I'd ever met that made me want to change my perspective on life and try to do better in every way that I truly could. She truly was a very special muse. Everything just always seemed so much better whenever she was around. I could really see us building a future together, with beautiful children, a house and a nice little garden.

The best thing about her was that she truly got me, like nobody else, and I understand her too, like no one else I had ever come across. After being numb for so long, she had taught me how to feel again, and it was very refreshing, just knowing I could be myself around her.

When I arrived at the restaurant, Joe was already there waiting for me. I sat down with him and the hostess came to take our order.

"Hey man, how are you doing?"

"Good, buddy, how are you getting on at work?"

She recognised us and gave us a nice smile. "Usual, boys?"

"Please," we both smiled.

"Thanks boys, I'll be back with your drinks soon."

She's cute. I love that she recognised us now too; she knew us far too well.

"Work is great, Joe. I've just been promoted again."

"That's amazing, man! So what do they call you now? Chief pen pusher?"

"Not quite," I replied. "I'm the Director of Studies."

"Sounds a little pretentious."

"Ha ha, I know it does, doesn't it? It makes for a nice little bit of extra cash in my bank though, so that's helpful, y'know? Plus I get my own office, with a plaque on the door too."

"Ooh fancy, Harrison!"

"I know, right? So what's new with you, Joe?" I asked. "You two must be excited about the baby?"

"Well, we're both pretty nervous, man. Although I think that Lisa is probably a little more enthusiastic than me."

"How so, Mr Architect?"

It was strange but nice to see how happy and scared he seemed at the same time, judging by the expression on his face. I hoped those two were prepared for the little one's arrival.

"I'm not sure, buddy. I'm just scared, y'know?"

"Joe, I can't say I've been there," I said, "but I'm sure it's perfectly normal to be a little scared. If you weren't, I would be worried. But I know this much: you two are going to be great together. Lisa is amazing, and I know that she will be a great mum, and you an amazing father, but more importantly, an incredible dad."

"Thanks Harrison. I'm sure it will be amazing when he gets here – tiring, but amazing."

"It will be, Joe," I said. "Everything will work itself out. It won't be easy, but you two will figure it out. I have every faith in you both."

"Thanks man. So what's going on with you and Amy lately?" he asked. "I know I've not seen you in a few weeks, but I figured today would be a nice chance to catch up with you."

"Ah Joe, she is *incredible.* I can't even begin to describe how great things are between us right now, man."

"Try, Harrison. I know that, for a man of few words, you sure like to talk a lot. Plus, it's great seeing you two together and it looks as though you're both truly happy too, which is amazing, man. It's almost as if she never left."

"We are Joe, we really are."

"She makes me feel really good about myself, you know? I feel as if I have a bigger purpose now, and a better reason for wanting to get out of bed."

That was all true too. Even now, after knowing Amy for this long, she still had that amazing effect on me. Whenever she walks into the room, I get chills all through my body, similar to when you hear a great line in a song, or your favourite band come out on stage for the first time.

That was a rush I could never tire of.

"I'm thinking about asking her to move in with me later tonight too. Whad'ya think, Joey boy?"

"Ah Harrison," he said, "you soppy old man. That's so awesome. Good luck – although I'm sure Amy would love the idea."

"Cheers Joe. It would be great."

"I'm so glad you've found someone you can be yourself around, Harrison. There is nothing in the world more valuable than that in a relationship. If you can't be yourself, then it's going to fail every time."

"Thanks Joe," I replied. "She's pretty amazing. I can see us growing old and fat together, maybe even a few grey hairs too."

"Do you think you'll stay in the same place?"

"Funny you should mention it. I am planning on moving into a new place – it's a little closer to work, in the middle of the city, with a view to die for. It sits on the tenth floor, overlooking the Southbank. I'm hoping to close the deal next week. You should come over and check it out, man. It looks incredible."

"That sounds awesome – at least you won't be stuck in the old place for much longer, especially if Amy moves in, y'know?"

"Yeah Joe, that would just be weird, wouldn't it?"

"I'll say," he said. "Too much has happened there."

The hostess came back with the drinks.

We smiled and thanked her.

"Joe?"

"Yeah, big man."

"This is weird being back here, you know?" I said. "The same restaurant with you and that same hostess who still looks as beautiful as she did when we were first here. Only now things are different: I'm sober, this morning anyway, the sun is shining, and everything is exactly how it should be. It's a new beginning."

"For both of us, things really couldn't be sweeter," he replied. "Just for the record though, that was super cheesy."

"Fuck you, Joe! You're buying the first round after breakfast for that."

"Just a quick one though," he said. "I gotta be back for Lisa."

"So, now that you're a partner in the firm, Joe," I said, "what does that mean, specifically? Do they give you a new set square?"

"Of course, Harrison. A silver one."

"Shit, that's awesome. I bet Lisa is so proud of you, Joe."

"I think she knows she's got a keeper, Harrison," he replied. "She should do too; I built the crib from scratch." He laughed; his talent knows no bounds.

"You are, after all, a grown man, and an architect no less."

"Well, Harrison, you're right, and a professional one too," he replied. "Architect, that is – not grown man."

"Exactly Joe," I said, "so you should really have a handle on it."

The food arrived, more quickly than normal; she must have put that order through as soon as we sat down.

"Here you are, boys."

"Thank you, that was quick!"

"I know. I put the order through as you walked in."

"Aw, that's so sweet of you. You are an absolute angel; we are starving!"

She smiled. "Enjoy, guys."

Nice girl, very sweet and, judging by the way she ran around this place, she earned every penny she made.

"Let's enjoy this nice little brunch and hit the Loch for a few cheeky ones. What do you think, Joe?"

"Sure thing, man," he replied. "Sounds good – let's do it!"

The food was good; you can't beat a nice bit of protein, and some caffeine – all great fuel for the body. Pre-beer was always a good plan on any day of the week.

We finished our food and left a nice tip for the hostess. "£10 on a £30 bill, why not? I'm feeling generous today. Plus, she works bloody hard for her money."

"I hear you, man."

"To the Loch, Joe!" I said, pointing to the sky.

"Usual then, Harrison?"

"Yes please, bro."

I ended up picking the seat near where we were before with all the Craig drama. "Ah, sweet memories! I'm so glad I don't have to deal with any of that shit anymore."

"I can only begin to imagine," Joe replied. "I bet you must be really excited for the next few months and what they will bring."

"Totally. I am really happy, you know, for the first time in a long while."

"It shows, Harrison, and that's great; you've certainly earned it, so soak it up, buddy, and make every second count."

"That's the plan, Joe. I think it's gonna be something beautiful."

"So, what have you got planned for tonight, Harrison? Anything special? Or are you two just having a quiet one?"

"In a sense, yeah," I said. "I was going to cook Amy something nice for when she comes back from town with the girls."

"Harrison in the kitchen – wow! Sounds nice, especially on a Saturday night. Who said chivalry was dead, eh?"

Damn right. "How about you two?"

"Nah man, just a quiet one. She's so pregnant right now. I can almost hear the baby screaming: why is daddy in the pub? I need feeding!"

"I bet you can, Joe, plus I know she'd kick your ass if she knew you were out late while she's at home prepping for the arrival of the little guy."

"You aren't far off, Harrison, that's true. I'd never see the sun again, and I like the sun, it makes me hopeful."

"Well, keep that in mind, won't you?" I said. "You have a great girl there, Joe, and you're both gonna do great. I'm sure of it, man."

"Thanks bro."

"You're welcome, Joe. Just don't fuck it up. If the home life is happy, and work is going great, then everything else is just noise. When everything is falling into place, sometimes we're too blind to see and it often passes us by because we're always chasing something bigger, and often, what we're looking for is right there in front of us, only a few are clever enough to see it though.

"More importantly, though, you should never settle, Joe, like so many other clichés, for anything – whether it be your job, or a relationship. If you can do better, then don't waste time. Make it fucking happen."

"Wow, that was pretty deep for a Saturday, Harrison, but true nonetheless; I want to do everything I can to make this woman happy and I'm sure I can do that."

"I know you will, Joe," I said. "You've got a huge heart and I know that you love the hell out of that woman."

I really did mean what I said too, and I hope he believed it; Joe is my oldest friend and I only wish him the absolute best and nothing less.

"Few people have that realisation," I continued, "where they have everything they would have ever dreamed of, and it's important to hold on to that; whether it's the job, girl or anything else. Life is painful enough as it is, and it's too short to worry about the past, and things that you can't change. That girl that you like and aren't sure if you should take a shot at, do it – life's too short for 'what ifs?'"

"Wow, Harrison, you're like some kind of owl, aren't you? But with more grey hairs!"

"Just a few, Joe. You're catching up, though!"

"It's gotta be your round, hasn't it?"

"Sure thing, Dad," I said. "Same again?"

"Damn, that sounds scary when you say it out loud, Harrison."

"Doesn't it just?"

"Please."

"So," I said, "have you given any thoughts as to what you're gonna call the little man once he's here?"

"Hmm, I'm not too sure yet, Harrison; Lisa likes Ozzie, but I prefer Logan. It seems badass."

"Yeah man, Logan is good. Very Rock 'n' roll too."

"I thought so too," he replied, "that's why I picked it. Hopefully, we can settle on that one."

"Well, good luck, Joe. I'm sure you can meet her somewhere in the middle."

"Have you mentioned to Amy about the move at all yet, buddy?"

"Yeah, she knows. I can't have us staying in the old place, far too much has happened there, and we can't start afresh in that kind of atmosphere, not with all that went down before, Joe."

"Change would be great too," he said. "After everything, a change of scenery would do you a lot of good."

"Damn right, Joe. The new place is a little more expensive, but so what? I work hard, why the hell shouldn't I enjoy my money a little?"

"We ought to get going soon, Harrison."

"You're right, Joe," I replied. "We'd best not keep our ladies waiting."

"True, we don't really wanna end the weekend on a low, do we?"

"Nah, Harrison."

"Drink up. Let's go."

"Alright buddy, I'll catch you soon, yeah?"

"Definitely, Joe."

"See you later, take care."

As I made my way back toward the flat, I took in the sights, and admired the beauty of the city. This little loch was like an oasis away from all the chaos, which was probably why we enjoyed coming here so much.

I had my mp3 player with me and thought I would put some miles on my new headphones too, so I threw some feelgood music on and strolled along, heading toward the bus station. Town was getting busy now, and everyone was out haggling with the market traders for some last-minute Saturday bargains.

I was never a huge fan of crowds, but I did like getting drunk. Although that was normally a team sport, it didn't require a large one. Sometimes, you can even play alone. Tonight, though, I have a nice bottle of red for Amy and I, and some beautiful food, which will be cooked by yours truly.

As I headed for the bus, I checked my watch and realised I'd spent a little too long admiring the city. I was going to be late home. I had better get my ass into gear; as quickly as I could move, though it was not quite quick enough for the Saturday shoppers.

Finally, I made it to the bus station, running along and trying to dodge the snail people. I nearly made it when the next thing I heard was –

BANG!

What the fuck was that?

What the hell was going on? Was the city under attack again!?

I guess I must have missed that bus coming toward me. After that, the last thing I could remember was feeling the cold tarmac pressed against my face and blood running down my neck.

I can barely make out the people rushing towards me, and then the ambulance, and now I'm in the ER. *This is it.*

All I could hear now was the incoherent noises and the stress of the doctors running around, frantically trying to save me, but I had that feeling again, in the worst way possible. *I had a bad feeling; I'd already lost far too much blood.*

I could just about make out what I thought was Joe and Amy in the background, Lisa too.

All of them were crying and pacing around like crazy.

I could just about make out Joe's voice saying "the doctors don't look happy; I don't know if he's going to win this battle".

I could feel Joe shaking me and screaming in my face.

"He can't fucking do this to me. He's never lost anything in his life! HARRISON!"

He was shaking his head, pacing up and down, while Lisa and Amy were in tears.

I could hear the doctors fighting over what to do next while waiting on some more units of blood.

He's not gonna make it. We need to act now!

We can still save this guy. He's lost so much blood already. Nurse, where's the O negative!?

"Please, I know you all care about this guy, but you have to let us work," a voice said. "You can't be in here, wait outside!"

Hurry, nurse!

"This guy's circling the drain. He's not going to make it!"

After what seemed like a lifetime of listening to the swarm of people in the ER fighting to keep me from going too soon, I realised that I felt nothing, no pain. I couldn't hear or feel.

Just silence.

That was it; it was over.

The only thing I could say I took from this was the fact that I'd finally found my perfect woman and she had been there all along.

Hiding in plain sight, disguised as my best friend.

Printed in Great Britain
by Amazon